THE WIFE OF A MIAMI BOY

A Hood Love Story

LAKIA

The Wife Of A Miami Boy

Copyright © 2020 by Lakia

All rights reserved.

Published in the United States of America.

All rights reserved. No part of this publication may be reproduced, distributed, or transmitted in any form or by any means, including photocopying, recording, or other electronic or mechanical methods, without the prior written permission of the publisher, except in the case of brief quotations embodied in critical reviews and certain other noncommercial uses permitted by copyright law. For permission requests, please contact: www.authortwylat.com.

This is a work of fiction. Names, characters, places, and incidents either are the products of the author's imagination or are used fictitiously. Any resemblance of actual persons, living or dead, businesses, companies, events, or locales is entirely coincidental. The publisher does not have any control and does not assume any responsibility for author or third-party websites or their content.

The unauthorized reproduction or distribution of this copyrighted work is a crime punishable by law. No part of the e-book may be scanned, uploaded to or downloaded from file sharing sites, or distributed in any other way via the Internet or any other means, electronic, or print, without the publisher's permission. Criminal copyright infringement, including infringement without monetary gain, is investigated by the FBI and is punishable by up to five years in federal prison and a fine of $250,000 (www.fbi.gov/ipr/).

This e-book is licensed for your personal enjoyment only. Thank you for respecting the author's work.

Published by Twyla T. Presents, LLC.

❦ Created with Vellum

ARE YOU ON THE LIST?

Click here https://bit.ly/2MO25jK
to join Twyla T. Presents' mailing list and receive new book release alerts, exclusive giveaways, sneak peeks & more!

Receive instant new book release alerts by texting TwylaT to 22828

1

JAYLA

"Damn, you been sportin' that rock for a few days now, when are you going to stop staring at it all the time?" Doe joked, gently placing his chin in the crook of my neck, tickling me with his beard.

His Gucci cologne invaded my nostrils and made me want to say fuck this random ass proposal party that Moochie was throwing me. Moochie was Doe's cousin and my best friend. When Doe popped the question on Sunday evening in our backyard while everyone was over for Sunday brunch, I was completely surprised and ecstatic. Once Doe slipped the ring on my finger, Moochie pulled me away to divulge the details of the ladies night she already had planned to celebrate our proposal. I never heard of a proposal party a few days after a nigga got down on one knee, but Moochie was always extra as hell so I didn't argue.

"Where do you think you're going smelling all sexy and shit?" I questioned with a raised eyebrow as I ran my perfectly manicured fingers through his beard.

"Well Meechie decided to throw a little something together for me since Moochie was doing something for you."

"And when exactly were you planning to tell me? After it was over?"

I quizzed with an attitude just that fast. I released the grip I had on Doe's beard as he stepped back. "You been moving real different lately Doe. Don't get fucked up now."

"Calm down Jayla, it's just a lil kickback. And I made it clear we didn't need any strippers, just some weed, liquor, and music, and I'm supa straight," Doe leaned in and kissed me on the lips before grabbing his keys off of the counter.

"Alright bae, but bring your ass home! I might be staying at the hotel with Moochie but you're a nigga. Y'all don't need to stay the night. Uber your drunk ass home if need be," I called out.

"I got you bae," Doe spoke and exited the front door.

I pulled out my phone and checked the time. It was already six o'clock, and I needed to shower and change into the dress Moochie dropped off for me earlier this morning. After showering and rubbing my body down with my favorite Nude Acacia body cream and gently spraying a few pumps of perfume on me, I was ready for the evening.

"Are you ready Ms. Jayla?" Raheem, my assigned bodyguard for the night, questioned from the opposite side of the bedroom door. "Moochie has been blowing up my phone for the past few minutes because you haven't answered for her."

"Tell her we are coming right now," I stood from the vanity and looked over myself in the floor length mirror one more time before I left the room.

Raheem was always so quiet but I liked it. The last nigga Doe had babysitting me talked too damn much. Raheem threw the keys to the valet driver before he opened my door and led me to the elevator of 1 Hotel South Beach. Moochie greeted us with a huge grin and a drink for me in her hand when she opened the door to the hotel room. Raheem stood outside the door while we went inside.

Moochie had really outdone herself with this one. All of our close friends and a few of my cousins were in attendance. There was a sexy female bartender in lingerie with a full liquor bar serving drinks. The treat table was covered in a Chanel theme, and I didn't waste any time eating a few chocolate covered strawberries. Moochie shoved another cup in my hand as soon as I finished the first one.

"Get ready to have some fun bitch!" Moochie yelled before she opened the door and a group of delectable male and female strippers entered the room.

Moochie turned the music up and the party really got started. I was placed in the chair in the middle of the floor while the strippers took turns putting on a show for me, and I allowed the dollars to flow freely. By the end of the night, the room was in shambles and Moochie and I were the last two left in the room. After eating and drinking into oblivion, I texted Doe to let him know that we were going to stay in the room and that Raheem would be in the room next door. Once he said it was cool, I climbed into the bed next to Moochie and passed out with her.

<hr>

"Wake yo ass up! I got shit to do today," Moochie woke me up from my sleep.

"What the hell you got to do? You had me turnt all night, now you trying to get rid of me. Some bestie you are," I flipped her my middle finger from the bed.

"I'm the best bestie around," Moochie threw a change of clothes at me, and I couldn't help but smile.

"I knew your ass didn't plan for me to go home once you said Raheem could just stay next door," I sat up in bed.

"I didn't. It has been so long since you let loose and lived. You have allowed Doe to turn you into a square ass bitch," Moochie teased.

"You introduced me to your cousin and now you want to complain. Girl, cut your shit. I'm going to shower and head home anyways. I need to make sure your brother ain't have Doe out doing too damn much last night," I referred to Meechie, Moochie's twin brother.

"Meechie, an ol' follow the leader ass nigga. Once he heard I was doing something for you, he started bugging me about where I was getting strippers from and shit so he could throw something together for Doe."

"Strippers?" I instantly caught an attitude.

"Girl relax. You had naked bodies in your face all night too."

"But I told that nigga no strippers and he assured me that there wouldn't be any in attendance!" I fumed, throwing the covers back and searching for my phone. "I'm about to fuck him and Meechie up."

"Uhhh no bitch, don't threaten my twin. Do whatever you please to Doe but leave Meechie out of it," Moochie quipped.

"Fuck both of them niggas," I yelped, snatching my phone from under the covers.

Before I could locate Doe's contact, I noticed all of the texts messages from my cousins and homegirls that were at the party last night. I ignored them thinking that they just wanted to discuss the wild events that took place last night. I felt slightly better when my phone started vibrating and the name *My Love* flashed across the screen.

"Doe..."

"Just relax and let me explain Jayla. I was fucked up and didn't mean for that shit to happen! Just come home so we can talk about it," Doe cut me off.

"What the fuck are you talking about Doe?!" I screamed into the phone as my eyes connected with Moochie's.

The look on her face let me know that she was well informed on whatever the fuck Doe was referring to. I hung up in his face without another word. My heart wasn't prepared for the screenshots that were sent to Moochie from a plethora of people. There my fiancé sat in the middle of whatever sleazy hotel they were in with his dick down a stripper's throat. I threw Moochie's phone to the wall and stormed over to Raheem's door.

BANG! BANG! BANG!

"I'm ready to go Raheem!" I screeched in the middle of the hallway.

BANG! BANG! BANG!

Shuffling could be heard on the opposite end of the door before Raheem exited the room, and I could see my baby cousin still asleep in his bed. I rolled my eyes and stomped down the hallway unable to address my cousin or Raheem at the moment. Moochie called out to me, but I was glad she was laying around in her bra and panties and couldn't chase me without taking a few moments to get dressed.

"I'm driving," I snatched the keys from Raheem the moment the valet attendant returned with his car.

This little Dodge Challenger was about to burn up these streets on the way to our home in Coconut Grove. The usual thirty minute drive was cut down to fifteen minutes the way I disobeyed all traffic laws. I swerved into my driveway and decided that this was it for me. Doe could take this ring and shove it up his ass!

"You alright Ms. Jayla?" Raheem questioned, following me up to the door.

"Fuck all y'all no good ass niggas!" I retorted before I damn near broke the door down unlocking it.

The fact that Doe's stupid ass didn't have enough sense to beat me home let me know that he was on some other shit, and he thought I was just going to get over his bullshit again. I quickly grabbed a duffle bag and stuffed a few outfits and all of my important documents inside. I could hear tires squealing in the driveway and the moment I looked out of the window, I could see Doe had blocked my car in with his.

"What the fuck you doing?" Doe snatched the bag out of my hand once I made it down the stairs.

"What the fuck does it look like? You letting strippers suck your dick in the middle of a crowded room for everybody to see. I don't want no nigga that shoots low budget pornos!"

"It ain't what it looks like. Them hoes were dancing and putting on a show and she just did that shit. I pushed her off of me as soon as I realized what was going on."

"He ain't lying sis. The strippers were on some other shit," Meechie appeared behind Doe, capping for his no good ass.

"Fuck both of y'all!" I yelled at the top of my lungs. "You said you told him no strippers, and I'm sick of this shit with your ass."

Meechie took that cue to head into the den and out of the foyer.

"Look Jayla, after last night, there ain't no more clubbing, no more partying, no more drinking unless you're on my arm. I swear bae. That's why I finally proposed after seven years of being together... I'm ready to really be the man that you need and deserve. I promise last night was my last fuck up," Doe pleaded.

I heard Doe but the shit wasn't moving me at the moment. Doe had put me through a lot of shit behind closed doors but for him to disrespect me publicly right after proposing to me spoke volumes. I knew Doe wasn't going to let me leave without a real fight. I still had Raheem's keys in my hands, so all I needed to do was get out of the door. If Doe thought his old trick of blocking my car would work today, he had another thing coming. Before Doe could blink, I picked up the vase off of the table up against the wall and used all of the strength in my body to crash Doe across the head with it. Doe involuntarily dropped my bag to cradle his injury, and I swiftly scooped it up and ran out of the door.

Raheem was standing outside on the phone oblivious to the situation at hand. I rushed past him and hopped into his car, locking the doors. Raheem rushed over and hit the window a few times.

"What is you doing Ms. Jayla?" Raheem questioned the moment I started the car.

Raheem pulled at the door handle a few times before he banged on the window.

"Please don't run off. You know that's going to land me in some shit," Raheem pleaded, but that wasn't my damn problem.

I put the car in drive and swerved out of the parking lot. All I could hear was Raheem screaming in the distance, and Doe calling out behind me as he chased the car down the street with his head leaking.

2

DOE

"Jaylaaaaaaaaaa!" I called out behind Raheem's car as it sped down the street.

"AGHHHHHHHHHH!" Raheem was screaming, jumping up and down, holding his foot. "Fuck! She ran over my fucking foot!"

"Good, how the fuck you let her run off in yo shit?" I bellowed, stomping over to Raheem as he sat on the ground cradling his foot.

"Calm down Doe," Meechie laughed, stopping me from putting hands on Raheem. "God damn she fucked both of y'all up."

"The shit ain't funny man! It's your fucking fault shit playing out like this. I told ya simple ass not to have no strippers there. I knew I should have kept my black ass home," I ranted. "Take this nigga to the hospital. I gotta go find my woman."

Meechie helped Raheem into his car and they skirted out of the driveway. I couldn't believe this shit. Just when I was really ready to turn my life around and settle down, shit went sour. Jayla was the love of my life the moment that I bumped into her at Moochie's house almost a decade ago when we were twenty three and twenty two. Jayla made me chase her ass for three years before she gave a nigga a real chance. Since she was a year older than me, fresh out of college, and in her own bag starting a successful nonprofit, she always played me to the left.

Jayla knew all of my secrets and was truly my best friend, and I couldn't lose her over some shit that really wasn't my fault. The shit I told Jayla was the God's honest truth. As soon as I cleaned my shit up and applied some pressure to my bleeding wound, I called Moochie.

The last time Jayla and I got into some shit, Moochie made me promise to keep her out of the middle of things, but I couldn't help it. I knew Jayla was probably venting to Moochie right now, and I needed to get to her. I was shitting bricks about this incident. No matter how mad Jayla got, she *never* packed a bag and left. Jayla was the queen of making me sleep in another room or making me get the fuck out of the house, but she *never* left our home since we moved in together five years ago.

After my fifth time calling Moochie with no answer, I tried my luck and dialed Jayla's phone number. I was quickly shot down when the automatic system went off in my ear.

"You have reached a number that has been disconnected or is no longer in service."

I threw the phone up against the wall and headed over to Moochie's house. She couldn't ignore me if I was standing on her doorstep. Once I pulled up to Moochie's house, I sent a text to Meechie to get the license plate information from Raheem and to have everybody's eyes looking out for his car and Jayla.

I used the emergency key that Moochie gave me to let myself in, and I instantly regretted my decision. The sight of Moochie sitting on the arm of her sofa while some nigga ate her box made me nauseous.

"Moochie!" I called into the house because she clearly didn't notice my presence.

"Nigga!" Moochie yelped and pulled her sundress down and over the nigga's head.

Once he found his way from under her dress and turned around, I realized it was Beanie, Raheem's older brother. Moochie was always fucking on the niggas on our team, so I didn't say shit. I just chunked up the deuces before he rushed out of the door.

"That key is for emergencies Doe! You letting a stripper suck your dick in the middle of the party and embarrassing my best friend isn't an emergency," Moochie paused and squinted her eyes in my direction. "Damn, Jayla fucked yo shit up. Serves you right," Moochie chuckled, grabbing a bottle of water out of the refrigerator.

"Yeah she bashed me over the head with a vase and skirted off in Raheem's whip. Oh, and not before she ran over his foot. Meechie is at the hospital with him right now," I expressed.

"Good for all of y'all no good asses. See y'all like to clown me at family functions for being a hoe and not having a man. But why have a man if he's going to be for everybody? I'll just keep shit cordial. I don't need the headaches that come along with you niggas."

"Fuck all of that Moochie, where is Jayla?" I questioned.

"Fuck if I know. The moment she saw those screenshots, she wouldn't talk to my ass either. I tried calling her but her phone says it's disconnected. You done really fucked up this time," Moochie advised me.

"I know, she packed a bag and everything cuz."

"Sounds like you have a real problem then," Moochie replied nonchalantly.

"Alright I see what this is cuz, you choosing sides and shit so let me slide," I pulled up my pants and headed for the door.

"Bye cry baby. Next time knock! You better be lucky he wasn't hitting it from the back or something when you barged up in my house."

After leaving Moochie's house, depression settled in quickly. The next day, I locked myself in the office to run numbers and told everybody to leave me the hell alone.

"We got a problem cuz," Meechie advised, stepping into the office.

"What's up man? I can't take no more bad news."

"Well get ready. I just left Beanie's crib and he has a suspicion that the trap Tone, Loc, and Bleezy run have came up short twice this month. He just wanted to make sure he was right before he told us because you know what happens next."

"How much short?"

"Shit, there was a brick missing two weeks ago and now this week, a second one disappeared."

"Usually, I want to make shit public but knocking them as an example might be a problem since Tone and Loc are the offspring of a few of the OG's, but they can't skate after this shit. What happened to that discreet nigga we had a few years ago?"

"I'm already on it," Meechie pulled out his phone and made a few calls.

Once I was alone again, I was lost in my thoughts as I had been over the last few days. After finishing up at the spot, I retreated to my empty kingdom for the second night in a row, feeling empty as hell. Two days turned into a week and before I knew it, an entire month had past and Jayla was still gone. I could barely eat or sleep and my business was beginning to take a dive behind it. I still hadn't made a move on the few niggas that tried the system. Since I was so torn up emotionally, I let the shit get out of hand and now, I needed to have some outside reinforcement come in and help out with the muscle.

3

JAYLA

"Jayla, where the fuck are you?" Moochie screeched into the phone. "Raheem still limping around with a fucked up foot, you got the boy on crutches and shit. Plus, they said Doe ain't left the house since you left."

"Not my problem… as long as my mama and daddy knew I was straight, that was all that mattered," I rolled my eyes at the thought of Doe.

"Oh just fuck me huh?"

"No bestie, but let's be real. Doe is your cousin and I already know that you were the first person Doe went crying to and shit. I don't like that," I retorted.

"I can't help it that we share the same grandma nah!"

"Yo bad, not mine."

"Stop being so cold bestie. When Doe came over here, I told him that he was dead ass wrong. I even laughed at the gash on the side of his head. I had your back bae."

"Ummmm hmmmmm. You saying that to me now, but you pick and choose when to respect the girl code when it comes to me and Doe. But I just wanted to check in and let you know that I'm straight. Once I find a place suitable for me, I will give you my location. But you have to earn that right by not giving Doe my new number. I'm really done with his ass this time."

"Okay bestie, don't take too long. I love you and everything will work out how it is supposed to."

"Thank you Moochie. I love you too, smooches," I cooed before I hung up the phone.

I laid back on the plush bed and scrolled through Facebook before I decided to leave the room for the first time since I checked into the hotel. I only brought two outfits with me, and I had been lounging around in one of the hotel robes since I got there. Retail therapy was definitely on my mind. It was funny that everybody thought I was long gone, but I just lowered my standards and stayed in a hotel that was cheaper. I knew Doe had checked every hotel that he would think I'd stay in. I threw on a pair of oversized shades and headed down to Brickell City Centre and grabbed a few things out of Saks and some undergarments from Victoria Secret before I was headed back to my hotel room to return to isolation.

Upon exiting the mall, my face was glued to my phone screen. This was the first time I opened my Facebook messenger app and Doe was in there laying it on thick. I left his ass on read as I felt myself hit a brick wall, causing me to drop my handful of bags. When I looked up, there was no wall, but my eyes connected with the sexiest piece of chocolate I had ever seen. He had to be at least 6' 2" and based off of our impact, he was definitely chiseled underneath his Jordan attire.

"My bad," I attempted to gather myself and stop salivating over the sight in front of me.

"You good. Let me help you," he grinned and bent down to grab my bags from the ground. "Where you parked at?"

"Ummmm right over here," I walked over to Raheem's car.

"Yo nigga let you borrow his whip, but he ain't here to carry your bags. You need to trade him in for a new one."

"That's where you're wrong, this ain't my nigga's car," I quipped, still smiling from ear to ear.

"Even better… that means you going to let me take you out. Once you let me in your life, I promise to always cover your shopping trips and carry the bags afterwards."

I contemplated my next decision for a moment. He was fine as hell, but I could tell he was young from his baby face. His simple outfit and the fact that he didn't know who I was let me know that he wasn't in the game. So I gave in and entered my number in his phone.

"Good. I have your number now. But I still don't want to let you out of my sight just yet. You should let me treat you to lunch, your choice."

I took a moment to think. I really wasn't trying to get caught up with another nigga. But I hadn't had an appetite since I left home, all of my meals had been forced fed. However, in that moment, I felt my appetite return and decided to give in to my stomach's desires.

"Okay, I think we can do lunch."

"My name is Q. What's your name?"

"My name is Jayla," I smiled.

Q gripped my hand and led me inside. We enjoyed a lovely meal filled with laughs and smiles. I don't think I'd ever smiled so much in my life. When I looked down at my buzzing phone, we had spent the entire day in the restaurant.

"I have really enjoyed this nice meal with you, but I need to get going. I've been here all day," I finally announced.

Q had paid for the check a few minutes ago, and I was feeling the effects of the alcohol so that was my cue to leave.

"Shit I understand. I'm way behind schedule as well," Q stood from the table and followed me out of the restaurant and to the mall's exit.

"So let me ask you something. How old are you?" My curiosity got the best of me.

"I'm twenty four, how about you?"

"I'm thirty three, see I knew you were a baby," I laughed.

"I ain't no baby, I'm a grown ass man. You just need to allow me to show you just how grown I am," Q lifted my hand and placed a gentle kiss on my hand. Butterflies instantly invaded my stomach, and if I were wearing any panties, they would have been soaked.

"Ummmm hmmmm. So where are you from? I've never seen you around."

"I'm from Miami. I moved to Tallahassee after I graduated from high school to attend FAMU. I graduated from FAM last week, and now I'm transitioning back home for a minute."

"Oh handsome and a good head on his shoulders," I noted verbally. "What did you go to school for?"

"Engineering, but I'm just taking a little break to make some cash before I go back for my masters. Grad school ain't cheap and I'm trying to really make some cash once I graduate."

"I really like the sound of that. I can't do nothing but respect a man with a plan," I flashed a flirty smile.

"So what do you do?" Q questioned, catching me off guard.

Truth be told, I wasn't doing shit but living off of Doe since the funding for nonprofits dwindled in out a few years ago. I would have had to pay out of pocket to continue to run my operation, and I didn't have the backing for that at the time. I didn't have an answer prepared, so I just threw some shit out there. Here I was calling him *a baby* when my shit was in shambles.

"I invested well after college, so I am kicking back with my feet up," I told half of the truth. I was kicking back with my feet up, but I was doing it off of Doe's dime.

"That's what's up, maybe you can show your boy something? I don't know shit about investing, but I know I want to be like you when I grow up."

"I got you. Now I'm going to head home and get myself together. I have a busy day ahead of me tomorrow," I lied to get myself away from Q.

Q might have been much younger than me, but he was so mature. Plus the fact that he wasn't in the streets and was trying to do something better with his life was exactly what I planned to look for in my next nigga.

"Let me grab the door for you," Q quickly reached in and opened the door to Raheem's car, and I took a seat as Q looked down at me, leaning over the car door.

"Alright Q. I need to get going," I reiterated.

"Call me and check in as soon you make it home," Q requested before he gently kissed my cheek.

"What, you my daddy now?"

"Nah, I ain't your daddy, but I'm definitely going to have you calling me daddy one day real soon," Q cockily grinned.

"Boy bye," I smiled and shut my car door before I started it and took off.

The entire ride home, I was reeling from the impromptu date between Q and I. I truly didn't plan to talk to him again though. He was too young for me. If I couldn't get Doe's ass to not fuck around behind my back, then I knew his young ass wouldn't be any different. The high I was on while with Q instantly disappeared the moment I sat my shopping bags down on the table in the hotel room. Three weeks had past and I needed to get my shit together and get out of this hotel wasting my money. However, I refused to tuck my tail and run back to Doe no matter what.

After finishing the ice cream, I hopped in the shower and changed into something comfortable. I pulled my tub of Ben and Jerry's ice cream out of the freezer and sat on the bed to watch *Bebe's Kids*. Once I was comfortable, my phone pinged and it was Q.

Q: I just wanted to make sure you made it home safely. I see you hard headed and that's okay. I like a challenge. Sleep tight beautiful. If you're up to it, I'd like to take you to breakfast in the morning.

"Fuck it, you ain't gotta marry the boy," I mumbled to myself.

Although I said I wasn't going to entertain him, his message sucked me right back in.

Me: I planned on ignoring you and never seeing you again. But you're in luck because breakfast is my favorite meal. What did you have in mind?

Q: Since breakfast is your favorite, you pick and I'll be there.

Me: Nah, I want you to pick. See where your head is since you're a grown man and all. Lol

Up until that moment, Q text me back instantly, but this time he left me on read. I sat the phone down on the bed and tuned back into the movie. Just as I started to get my laugh on, my phone rang.

"Hello," I quickly answered when I saw Q's name flash across the screen.

"See, we about to get some shit straight right now. I'm a *grown ass man*, I do *grown ass things,* and I can take care of *my grown ass woman*. So all them sideways jokes gone stop. Since I am a grown man, I'm going to keep it real with you. We are staying in the same hotel, so you should just come to my room in the morning and allow me to prepare a home cooked breakfast for you."

"H...hu...huh?"

"Yeah, I saw your non driving ass swerve into the parking lot before me about an hour ago... that's how I know you had time to get settled in and you just chose to ignore my request to check in. That car can't be yours. You don't know how to control the speed in that bih. So I'm going to ask you again. Is that your nigga's car?" Q caught me off guard, but I bounced back fast.

"That ain't my nigga's car!"

"You stay in the hotel with yo nigga?"

"No Q! If you really want to know, I just left my nigga three weeks ago. That's why I'm staying here."

"Damn, I'm sorry to hear that. But that nigga's fuck up is where I'm about to luck up. So you coming to my room for breakfast in the morning?"

"Let me think about it. I don't know you like that to be in your hotel room," I answered.

"Ain't nobody going to hurt yo ass," Q shot back.

"Alright. I'm going to come to your room as soon as I get up in the morning. What room are you in?"

"213. What do you want for breakfast? I'm going to run to Walmart real quick."

"I like pancakes, bacon, and eggs. You know any traditional breakfast combination. Your ass better be able to cook because if you can't, I won't ever let you live this shit down," I joked.

"You'll see. Now, I'm going to cook breakfast and you going to make dinner. So what you trying to make your boy?"

"When did I agree to that?" I inquired.

"Don't tell me you're one of those grown ass women who don't know how to cook."

"Q, don't play with me. My mama taught me how to maneuver

around the kitchen. You grab whatever you want for dinner and I will make it. How about that?"

"Sounds like a plan to me. Let me hit Publix and I'll see you in the morning Jayla. Sleep tight."

"Good night Q."

4
Q

Watching the taillights on Jayla's car disappear was hard because I didn't want to let her go. Her smile was infectious and her aura was definitely alluring. The thing that really had me feeling Jayla was the very thing that had her playing me to the left, our age difference. Most of these bitches my age only cared about bundles, Fashion Nova outfits, nails, and likes on Instagram. I wanted a woman who was into her bag and bringing more than just a pretty face to the table.

After leaving the mall, I headed back to my hotel room and knew I would have full access to Jayla when she whipped the Challenger across the intersection in front of me, damn near causing an accident. If it would have been anybody else, I would have followed them to their parking spot and snapped on their ass. But I observed Jayla's movement into the hotel room to see if she was there with her nigga.

After hanging up the phone with Jayla, I hit Walmart and Publix to grab everything that we would need for tomorrow. I planned on really showing out with my cooking skills. The sound of my ringing phone tore me away from my slumber. It was 8:30 and Jayla was calling me before I woke up. That shit had me smiling from ear to ear.

"Hello," I put on my best voice to pretend to be awake.

"You up grown man?" Jayla questioned sarcastically.

"I been up. I'm just waiting for you," I lied.

"Ummm hmmm, well why have I been knocking on your door without receiving an answer for the past few minutes?" Jayla chuckled.

"Alright, you caught me. Here I come," I stood from the bed in my Polo pajama pants with my bare chest exposed and went and opened the door.

Jayla stood there with her hair wrapped up in a scarf, wearing a PINK pajama set. Jayla's eyes eagerly roamed my body until I finally spoke up.

"Are you just going to stand there and gawk all day or are you going to come in?" I questioned, already standing to the side giving Jayla access to enter the room, but she was too busy eye fucking me.

"Boy bye," Jayla waved me off and walked into the room.

"I got eyes, I can see Jayla," I closed the door behind her. "Make yourself comfortable. Since you know I just woke up, I need to brush my teeth and take a piss. I'll be back."

I walked into the bathroom and relieved my bladder, washed my hands and face before I brushed my teeth. I checked my Colgate smile in the mirror before I walked back into the small dining area that Jayla was seated in with her face buried into her phone, smiling from ear to ear. I crept around the side and snatched the phone out of her hand and locked both of our phones in the safe.

"What the hell do you think you're doing?" Jayla sassed once she gathered herself.

"I'm ensuring that I have your undivided attention while we are together and you will receive the same from me."

"I'm going to play by your rules, but if my phone rings back to back, I'm checking my shit."

"As I will do the same," I nodded my head in agreeance and swiftly placed a gentle kiss on her cheek.

"I promise you are truly winning me over too fast. I might need to take my ass back to my room," Jayla giggled.

"That's all I'm trying to do. Once you taste this breakfast, I'm going to have you hooked," I wrapped my arms around Jayla from behind as she sat on the stool.

"We will see. Now get them pots rocking. I'm hungry," Jayla pushed me towards the kitchen.

"Would you like a mimosa while you wait?" I pulled one of the wine glasses out of the cabinets.

"Boy stop sounding like my waiter. But yes I would. Let me find out you're a bartender," Jayla cracked a smile.

I pulled the orange juice, strawberries, and champagne out of the fridge and practiced what I watched on YouTube videos last night. The look on Jayla's face following her initial sip let me know that I had done my job. I silently celebrated my victory and returned to the kitchen and prepared breakfast while Jayla and I talked about everything under the sun. After breakfast was done, Jayla was also impressed by my cooking skills.

We spent the next few hours lounging around in my hotel room until Jayla suggested we go to the poolside bar downstairs. Jayla went back to her room and got changed, and I walked over once I was changed. Jayla and I were only staying a few doors down from each other, so we were destined to run into each other. I'm just mad we hadn't crossed paths sooner.

Sitting across from Jayla at the bar, I couldn't help but take in her flawless brown skin and her natural hair up in a high bun. The light pink bathing suit holding up the perfect set of perky titties that she possessed had me turned on without her doing anything.

"OMG... please don't *ever* lick your lips like that again," Jayla interrupted my thoughts. "I don't *ever* want to be with a nigga who has any similarities with that fool."

"Well damn ma. I can't help the way I lick my lips. I have been doing that since I was a young boy. What ol' boy do to have you that moved by something so simple as me licking my lips? I'm going to listen to this shit one time, then you gotta forget about his ass and worry about your future with me."

"He cheated time and time again. All of his apologies and changed behavior for a few months were always just an act to suck me back in so he could do the same thing over and over again. But I'm too old for that shit now," Jayla vexed. "I promise that is going to be the last time I bring my ex up. You're right, I have to worry about my future."

"With me," I added.

"We will see."

"How he did you was fucked up. But I can assure you that I'm nothing like that nigga. Once you're over him and *really* ready to move on, I promise to show you that. Now don't get yourself all worked up over a fuck nigga that didn't know what he had in front of him. I recognize your value, and I promise to prove it to you everyday if you let me."

"Baby steps," Jayla's mood changed for the better with that answer. "We will see where things go."

Jayla and I spent the rest of the day together. Everything was fun and easy going with her. After swimming in the pool and sipping on a few drinks, Jayla cooked a mini feast for dinner. The fried chicken, macaroni and cheese, broccoli, and biscuits reminded me of my mother's cooking, so I knew Jayla could throw down.

We spent the rest of the night talking about everything you could think of until we fell asleep. I woke up in the middle of the night with Jayla snoring in my arms on the couch and Netflix paused asking, *Are you still watching*? I gently placed a kiss on Jayla's forehead and carried her to the bed. Jayla stirred a few moments before she got comfortable and went right back out. I laid back on the couch and went back to sleep. I was the perfect gentleman, which usually wasn't like me, but I wanted something different with Jayla.

I woke up the next morning to Jayla wearing a completely different outfit, letting me know she went back to her room and came back. The breakfast she was cooking had my stomach rumbling, so I went to the bathroom and handled my hygiene. When I returned, Jayla had our plates set on the table. I placed a kiss on her cheek and grabbed the glasses from her hand and took them to the table for her.

Jayla's breakfast tasted just as good as the dinner she made last night. Her cooking skills alone made me want to wife her up even more. From that day forward, we were stuck under each other for the next three weeks we stayed in the hotel. My place was finally ready and

I was moving out of the hotel room the next day, but I wasn't happy to be moving away from Jayla.

"I'm moving out tomorrow. So what's up with you getting into a place? You can't stay here forever, plus you moving on with a new nigga," I flashed a smile.

"I have been looking, and I like a few places I've viewed. I plan to make a decision really soon."

"If you can't find anything, you should come stay with me and save money until you find what you're looking for," I offered before I placed a kiss on the back of Jayla's neck as we laid in the bed.

"I appreciate the kind gesture for real. But I don't want to put myself in that situation with another man so soon. I'm going to find a place soon, I promise," Jayla voiced and turned over to face me.

Jayla's tongue invaded my mouth for the first time since we had been seeing each other. We were laying in bed watching Netflix, so I couldn't help but to brick up in response to Jayla's gesture. Since we started kicking it three weeks ago, we hadn't crossed the line of pecking. I was being respectful due to the fact that I really wanted something with Jayla, and I knew she was fresh out of a toxic relationship.

But the moment Jayla straddled me, it was over from there. Our tongues and bodies were intertwined simultaneously. Jayla took complete control, pulling my dick out from my boxers and straddling me. I gripped her hips as she gently slid down on my pole. Jayla bounced up and down with the perfect rhythm; the fact that I hadn't had none since we met had me fighting my urge to bust too quick. Jayla already had an issue with our age, so I had to gain control and make our first time something to remember.

I wrapped Jayla up in my arms and spun her around and administered straight back shots until she was yelping my name in both pleasure and pain.

"Nah grown woman... stop running," I pulled Jayla back into me and kept at the same pace.

"B...boy, I don't run," Jayla tried to articulate between strokes.

Jayla still tried to run again, so I followed her until she couldn't run any further without going through the headboard. Once I started rubbing Jayla's clit, she caught my rhythm and started throwing it back until we both reached that place of ecstasy. Jayla collapsed on the bed and I gently placed a kiss on her lips, and Jayla rolled over so we could be face to face.

"You earned grown man status now. No more little boy," Jayla grinned, and I took the lead and initiated round two.

5

JAYLA

I woke up the next morning feeling better than I had since I left Doe. I guess I needed that orgasm more than I realized. Q didn't know but he had me hooked off of that bomb dick. We went at it until we passed out around three in the morning. I woke up cooking, cleaning, and rethinking Q's offer. Maybe staying with him until I found a spot and saved some money wasn't such a bad idea. I heard Q stir from the bed once I got the pots on the stove.

I was now comfortable enough to walk around in my bra and panties, and Q clearly was comfortable as he walked over to me. When I say his dick was swanging, it was *swanging*. Q pressed up against me and placed a kiss on my lips. I didn't even mind that he hadn't brushed his teeth yet in that moment.

"Bae, put that thing away and brush your teeth, breakfast is almost ready," I instructed.

"A nigga *bae* now, so I'll gladly follow directions," Q walked off with a cheesy grin.

I finished stirring the eggs and shoveled them onto the plates with the bacon and toast. Q returned with his hygiene in order and grabbed the orange juice and two tall glasses to assist me. We sat down at the table and quietly ate our meals. I know I was acting a little shy after how nasty we got last night, but I could tell that Q was just hungry from the way he devoured his breakfast, almost had *me* ready to get ate again. I quickly pulled my mind out of the gutter once we were done with breakfast.

"I got the dishes today," Q stood up and grabbed the plates off of the table and headed into the kitchen. "I have to meet my realtor in an hour to grab my keys and then if you want, I can come back to pick you up and show you the place."

"Okay," I walked around the room, gathering our items from the previous night since Q already had the few items he had here packed up near the door. "I was thinking Q, maybe I will take you up on that offer and stay with you and save a little money. But this isn't permanent. I'm just staying until I find a place."

"I understand, maybe I can set you up with my realtor so she can help you. She's A1, I promise," Q walked over and grabbed the clothes from my hand and kissed me on the cheek. "So go get packed. I'll be back in a few hours. I'm going to hit the grocery store and grab some food, so I can cook dinner for my woman in my new place tonight."

"Okay bae," I pecked Q on the lips and headed towards the door. "I might need a little extra time. My best friend is stopping by to bring a few of my things today. Send me the address and I will come over once I'm finished. I can have someone here carry my bags to the car."

"Alright bae," Q yelled before I left.

I went back to my room and packed up the few things I had there. I wasn't sure what was in store for Q and I, but he had been nothing but the perfect gentleman since we met. I was usually the type of person who planned every little detail about my future, but I said "fuck it, I'm living in the moment."

Once everything was together and ready for me to slide out, I pulled out the control and flipped through the channels while I waited for Moochie. I was in such a rush to get away from Doe that I forgot to grab my most prized possession, my MacBook; it had my entire life on it. Moochie was gracious enough to swindle it from the house I previously shared with Doe a few weeks ago, but I had been so caught up with Q that I hadn't had a moment to grab it from her. Plus I was still riding in Raheem's car, so I didn't want to be on that side and risk anybody seeing me.

After dozing off while texting Q, I woke up to a light knock at the door. I jumped up excited to see my bestie because I truly did miss her. As soon as I swung the door opened, Moochie started barking down the hallway.

"Oh hell no! What the fuck you doing here?" Moochie yelled down the hallway before she turned back to me. "I didn't tell him you were here Jayla, I swear."

I didn't need to look down the hallway. I already knew it was Doe's sleazy ass. I grabbed Moochie's arm to pull her inside, but before I could slam the door, Doe stuck his foot in the way.

"What you in such a rush to shut the door for? You got a nigga in here?" Doe entered the room and pulled his gun off of his waist.

"No, community dick! That's more your speed. Get out Doe, we are done!"

"Moochie, can you give us some time alone? I ain't seen my woman in six weeks now," Doe completely ignored my request.

"Hell no! Doe, you're leaving, Moochie, you're staying!"

"I'm not trying to get in the middle of y'all shit. I'm just going to go," Moochie muttered and backed out of the room.

"I knew your ass was lying, you brought this nigga here!" I screeched and Moochie's guilty ass kept walking out of the door before I turned my attention to Doe. "I swear to God Doe, you need to follow her out! I don't have shit to say to you. I'm ready to move on and find real happiness that doesn't come along with thot cock," I burned him with a new line I heard from a song somewhere.

"Jayla, please calm down and hear me out. I promise that I didn't let that bitch suck my dick! I promise I'm ready to change," Doe spoke gently and walked over to me and quickly wrapped his arms around me. "I swear I can't lose you. Look at me, I'm losing weight and shit... I can't eat, I can't sleep. You have proven your point. Just come home Jayla, I miss ya ass."

"I'm not coming home. Like ever... we are DONE!"

"You are coming home and you coming home *now*. Come on Jayla, you been down with me since I got started in the game, you been there through the struggle and the come up. Do you really want to let another bitch come along and reap all of the benefits and all of the work you put in? I know you love me and I love you. I never want to lose you, so I promise to never fuck up again. We can go down to the courthouse and get married today. Anything you want Jayla."

I couldn't lie, I still loved Doe. We had been together for so long and he was all that I knew as an adult. No, I didn't want to ex him out of my life, but I wanted to feel secure in my relationship.

"I'll do anything," Doe dropped down to one knee and started singing Avant's parts of *My First Love*.

As mad as I wanted to be, I couldn't help but smile at Doe and his antics. All of that shit Doe said didn't move me; it was the thought of moving on and getting into new things that scared me. Once Doe was done singing, he stood up and kissed me on the lips and I didn't fight him off.

"Okay Doe, I'm going to come home, but shit is going to be under my terms," I conceded. "I'm not having sex with you until I'm ready and your nasty ass has to get checked first. If you ever have me out here looking stupid again, I'm leaving and never looking back, so please agree to leave me the fuck alone. I'll start planning the wedding and I'm getting everything I want with no budget."

"Whatever you want Jayla."

"One more thing," I paused. "I want 100K in my bank account right now. So if things don't work out, I will have money to get myself together and ensure that I'm straight."

"100K?" Doe question.

"Yeah nigga, 100K! Like you said, I have been there from the start. That's the least I deserve! That's not a lot of money to you. If you don't think I'm worth that, then fuck it."

"I'm with it. Let's just get home, I can't wait to get you home," Doe excitedly grabbed my things and headed for the door.

"No, I want my money right now. So make whatever calls you need to make," I planted my feet in the middle of the floor and folded my arms across my chest.

"Alright Jayla... fuck."

The fact that Doe agreed to my final demand shocked the hell out of me. Once I confirmed the money was in my account, we headed out of the hotel room. I paused for a moment and thought about Q. I couldn't lie; that was some of the best sex I ever had and I did like him. However, the way that I immediately melted under Doe's touch showed me I wasn't ready to move on, and it wasn't fair for me to have him caught in the middle.

6
JAYLA

Since I came home, Q has blown up my phone day in and day out. He texted and called a few times every day. Q even asked me to just let him know that I was *okay* a few times, but I couldn't bring myself to do so. I couldn't bring myself to break things off right after I told him I would move in with him. This was my second week home and I finally changed my phone number before Doe noticed the constant calls and texts from Q. Doe had been on his best behavior, but I was still on my toes and ready to bounce at the first sign of some bullshit.

"Bae, I booked you a spa day and a car to take you there," Doe came into the kitchen and informed me.

"Really?" I questioned because this wasn't like Doe; he never did romantic shit like this.

"Really, I told you I'm a changed man," Doe placed a kiss on my cheek because I revoked his privilege of feeling my lips the moment we got back home.

I wasted no time getting showered, changed, and into the car. We pulled up to my favorite spa, and I immediately knew Moochie had to help him plan this shit. I didn't care though; she was still getting the silent treatment for telling Doe where I was and trying to lie about it.

She really showed me where her loyalty lied. I walked inside and decided to have the massage first. Once I changed into my robe, the door to my room opened up and Moochie walked in wearing a robe as well.

"Oh hell no! I knew you had to help him plan this, but I didn't expect you to be bold enough to show up here," I ranted.

"Stop Jayla! I had to take him, this nigga was losing his mind. He was stalking me and blowing up my phone like I was his woman. Then he took it to another level and started showing up at my house randomly while I'm trying to get my rocks off. Plus, you wasn't leaving him. Jayla, y'all have been together for far too long and you have been there through the ups and downs of this business, ain't no way you was leaving and letting the next bitch step in and reap the benefits of the nigga you helped mold. He is your first and only. Plus, Meechie told me that Doe wasn't lying; the stripper really did just pull his dick out and he pushed her off."

A piece of Moochie's speech sounded just like Doe and now I was wondering if she helped him prepare that speech he gave me. The fact that Doe wasn't lying about the stripper didn't move me; he still embarrassed me. My anger began to rise and before I knew it, I blurted out a secret I planned to take to the grave.

"He ain't my only no more," I bragged before I had the chance to stop my quick tongue.

"Say whattttttttttttt? I should've known that's why you wasn't giving me the time of day during your little escape."

"You got damn right. The only reason that I considered reconciling with Doe is because I had enough time to do me and feel good."

"I need all the details," Moochie rushed over and sat on the other massage table.

"I can't lie, he was everything. He was tall, dark, and handsome. Plus, he had a perfectly chiseled body, and he was the sweetest. I was supposed to move in with him until I found me a new place. Untilllll your ass brought Doe to my hotel room," I explained.

"Oh Jay, y'all was in deep," Moochie chimed in. "How was the sex?"

"Bitch, it was A1. I was so shocked the way his young ass put it down, plus he wasn't scared to eat it unlike your cousin," I stuck my tongue out.

"Young? How young bih?"

"He was only twenty four."

"You say it's because of my age girl, but age ain't nothing but a number," Moochie started singing Pretty Ricky's version of the song. "I love me a young bull. If he was all that, why the fuck you come back to Doe?"

"I really don't know."

"Was he broke?" Moochie continued her line of questioning.

"He just graduated from college with a bachelors in engineering and is planning to work for a little before he returns for his masters. He had enough money to look out for me, so I'm sure he got a little something but clearly not as much as Doe. But it wasn't about the money; the only thing that had me hesitant was his age. I was worried about competing with these young hoes though," I confessed.

"Fuck them! You a bad bitch at thirty three, you look better than these smoked and fucked out young bitches," Moochie cackled.

"Well I would probably be fucking him right now if you wouldn't have brought your cousin back to me."

"Girl, y'all have been locked away in the house in marital bliss until today."

"I love Doe, I truly do. But I don't know. I'm trying to make shit work between us, but I don't know if too much damage has been done. I was giving this shit my best foot forward, but then you came in here and made me realize that this nigga either stole your lines or you fed him all of the lines he came into my hotel room spitting. Every day, I realize I really only know the best side of Doe, but he has a whole other side that's a straight fuck nigga."

"Alright, enough of this love life talk. If you want Doe, be with Doe. If you want the young boy, go be with the young boy. What did you say when you cut him off?"

"I didn't cut him off, I just ghosted him."

"Girl, what are you, twelve? You are too damn old to be ghosting people," Moochie grabbed her chest.

"I know, but I couldn't formulate the proper way to break things off with him and the more calls I missed, I lost my courage and just said fuck it. Let it stay where it lies."

"Jayla, act your age and call that man and end things properly. Here I was thinking you changed your phone number because of me; this entire time, you running from another nigga that you're hiding from Doe. I say keep him on standby just in case Doe fucks up again."

Just like that, Moochie's fucked up choices were absolved and we were back thick as thieves. After getting full body massages and pedicures, we went out to lunch before we parted ways. Moochie had Q on my mind heavy for the rest of the day, but it was too late to turn around now. When I fell asleep next to Doe that night, I couldn't stop the flashbacks of the one night of sex Q and I shared, and I almost wanted to give Doe some just to quell my desires; but I stood firm and went to sleep in his arms. We had to be up early the next morning to meet with the wedding planner anyways.

The next morning, Doe and I were dressed and sitting in the back of the suburban as Raheem maneuvered through traffic to our destinations today. Our first stop was the wedding planner, Nina's office, to review our budget, dates, and general ideas before we moved to the next step in the process.

"Hello," Nina greeted us both with a handshake.

"Hello," I replied before I took a seat across from her and Doe sat next to me with my hand encased in his.

"So let's start with the most important piece of planning a wedding. What's your budget?"

"$200,000." Doe spoke up.

"Ummmmm, no it's not. You said I wouldn't have a budget. Those were your words Doe," I turned to him with an attitude.

"We not about to spend over 200 grand on a damn wedding. Hell nah," Doe retorted.

This was typical Doe, reeling me in just to dick me around. But this time, a new bitch was in town, and I wasn't here for the bullshit. I didn't plan to spend that much money. I wasn't that stupid; however, I didn't like him going back on his word yet again.

"Well marry your damn self!" I stood up and marched out of the office.

Doe came out calling my name, but he had me fucked up if he thought he was going to pull the same shit he always did. I made sure the elevator shut before he could reach it and rushed to the car.

"Take me home now Raheem," I ordered once Raheem opened the door.

"What about Doe?"

"Are you my driver or Doe's driver?" I snapped.

Raheem didn't reply; he hopped in the car and peeled off. I could see Doe rushing out of the office, but I didn't give a damn as long as Raheem didn't see him and kept his foot on the gas. I looked down at Doe's ringing phone in my hand and laughed to myself. Doe was going to feel me for everything he put me through. The same number called back again and this time, I answered, prepared to curse any bitch out, but it was Doe's lucky day because it was his dumb ass.

"Where the fuck you at Jayla? I paid the retainer fee just to secure this meeting and you done stormed out and shit."

"You told me I could have whatever I wanted. If you didn't mean that shit, I can go back to my hotel," I barked into the phone.

"Alright Jayla, it's whatever you want. Now tell Raheem to turn around and come get me. You got my phone and I don't know anybody number by heart."

"Nah, we almost home. You a grown ass man. Figure it out," I hung up in Doe's face before I laughed to myself.

"Everything straight Ms. Jayla?" Raheem questioned as he pulled onto our block.

"Everything is fine Raheem."

"Cool. Since I have you alone Ms. Jayla, I found this in my car," Raheem held up Q's ID and my heart sank to the pit of my stomach.

"I don't know who this belongs to," I quickly played dumb.

"Oh, I found it in my car when I got it back. I assumed it belonged to someone you knew," Raheem mentioned.

"Nope, not me," I ended the conversation.

I wasn't about to give Raheem nothing to hold over my head. I don't even know why this two plus two ass nigga had the nerve to bring that shit to me; the foot injury must have his head fucked up. My mood was completely thrown off once I stepped out of the truck. I threw Doe's phone on the bed and put back on my pajamas before I curled up under my blanket. It was too hot outside to be trying to take off on Doe and head to Moochie's house, so I just wanted to nap under the AC. Just when my body slipped into that good REM sleep, the sound of my bedroom door slamming shut woke me up.

"I know you saw I was sleeping," I sat up with an attitude.

"Jayla, you got me fucked up. I know that I have made some mistakes, but you been giving me hell since you got back. How long you think I'm supposed to take this shit? You didn't even give me a second to work shit out today and we lost out on some money."

"As long as I feel like it Doe. If you don't like my attitude, fix your actions. Now if you would excuse me, I'm going back to sleep."

"Alright Jayla, you and your fucked up attitude scared the little white lady off. You're going to have to find another wedding planner because now, she claims that she's booked up for consultations for the next few months. If you wouldn't have hung up on me, you would have known that and brought your ass back."

"I wouldn't have," I threw the covers over my head and tuned Doe out.

The next day, I made an appointment to meet with another wedding planner since we acted an ass in front of Nina. Doe and I attended the meeting the following week and I was able to make all of my preliminary requests for venues and themes. After the meeting, we had a nice quiet meal, and for once, Doe made me feel bad for all of the hell I was causing since I came home.

"We have to get some sort of understanding Jay," Doe gripped my hand. "How are we supposed to make things work if we can't get on the same page? I understand you want to hurt me just as much as I've hurt you, but how is that going to get us to the next level in our relationship?"

"I don't know," I mumbled before guzzling down the rest of my drink. "I guess you're right."

"So are you ready to give us a fair chance or are you ready to be done with this?"

Doe's last statement caught me off guard for sure. The fact that he seemed ready to let me go said that he was really over my antics and it was time to put them to rest.

"I'm sorry for my behavior, and I'm really ready to try to make this work. But you're still going to follow my rules. I'm just going to try my best to have a better attitude."

"Okay, I love you Jayla and we are going to be straight. Now I gotta make a move with Meechie. Raheem can take you home, and Meechie is coming to scoop me now," Doe stood from the table, placing a hundred dollar bill on the table and kissing me on the cheek.

"Okay Doe, I love you too."

7
JAYLA

After the come to Jesus dinner with Doe, I stopped being childish and we really got our wedding planning on the road. I decided that I wanted to have a country club wedding and all of our family and friends were invited. After meeting Draya, our new wedding planner, to look at color schemes and centerpieces, Doe headed back home while I went to the mall for some retail therapy. After we were done shopping, Raheem carried my bags back to the car while Moochie and I texted to make plans for a girls night.

"I'm so sorry Ms. Jayla, I need to run back in to take a piss," Raheem announced.

I rolled my eyes but luckily, I wasn't in a rush so I didn't mind too much.

"I'm just going to sit here."

"Okay. I'll be fast," Raheem rushed out of the car and to the entrance.

I was clicking around on Facebook for a few moments when the passenger door on the opposite side of the car swung open.

"So where you been hiding out?" I looked up and Q was standing in the doorframe with the meanest glare I had ever seen.

"I... I'm sorry Q."

"Yeah, yeah, yeah. You got back with that nigga I see. But you could've had the decency to let me know what was up. Instead, I was around here stressing and guessing. That's the lame ass nigga you wanna be with?"

"That's not my nigga," I answered. "But I am working things out with my man, Q. I'm sorry, you're completely right. I should have been honest with you but I couldn't. I had feelings for you, and I didn't want to let you down."

"You had feelings, but you'd rather run back to the nigga that showed you he ain't shit time and time again? That makes sense?" Q got sarcastic, but I didn't have the time. I needed him to get the fuck on before Raheem came back and recognized his face from his ID that was left in the car.

"You done Q? Because your antics ain't moving me, you're a little boy and I need a grown man," I tried to cut him deep so he would get gone and stay gone.

Q started laughing hysterically before he slammed the door shut. I closed my eyes and laid my head on the seat. I made a mental note to curse Raheem the fuck out for not locking the doors. The sound of the driver's door opening made my eyes pop open; just as I was about to give it to Raheem, I realized it was Q's ass in the driver's seat. Q backed out of the parking spot at full speed.

"What the fuck are you doing?" I yelled as Q swerved out of the parking lot, ignoring my question. "Q! What the hell... you kidnapping me?"

"You sound dumb as fuck Jayla! Don't nobody have to kidnap your ass. Just sit back there and shut up unless you about to hop out of this bitch!"

I actually did consider hopping out a few times, but I decided against it. I felt like I could trust Q to keep me safe, even if he was a lover scorned. After driving a few minutes, Q pulled into the driveway of a cute little house and killed the engine.

"Get out!" Q ordered.

I rolled my eyes and followed his commands. I didn't have any idea what Q had in mind, but I decided to go with it. As soon as I stepped out of the car, Raheem started calling my phone.

"Hello," I quickly answered so he wouldn't alert Doe to my disappearance.

"Where you at? I could have sworn we parked right out front," Raheem noted.

"I had to make a run. I will be back to get you in a minute," I replied.

Before Raheem could respond, Q snatched my phone and disconnected the call.

"I only need a few minutes of your time Jayla and then you can get back to your life," Q voiced and shoved my phone in his pocket.

Q grabbed my hand and led me up the walkway to the front door. Once inside, I took in the ambiance and I had to say the house was cute. Much smaller than the home I shared with Doe, but it was still nice. Q continued down the hallway and into the first bedroom on the right.

"I did this for your ass," Q announced as he opened the door.

The room was painted coral, which was my favorite color. There was a cute oversized vanity against the left wall and the right wall had a huge floor length mirror.

"Once I left the hotel room, I had some boys come over and put all this shit together for you. I listened to you talk about the makeup room you wanted when you moved to a new place. I remembered your favorite color the first time you said it. But you chose a nigga that can't remember your favorite color or favorite meal after being together for damn near a decade. I just wanted to show you your loss when you passed up a nigga like me," Q walked out of the room and I quickly followed suit.

"I'm sorry Q," I faltered as we stepped outside.

"You good Jayla," Q handed me the keys and slammed the door in my face.

"Fuck you Q!" I shouted and marched back to the truck.

During the ride back to the mall, Q's words resonated within me because he was right. I had admitted to Q that Doe rarely knew the small things about me and that was also one of my issues with our relationship. Raheem was standing outside of the entrance pacing back and forth like his life was over, but it was his lucky day because I brought my ass back to get him.

"What happened to you? I was worried as fuck!" Raheem rushed over to the driver's seat and I quickly hopped in the back. "You good? What happened?"

"I got my period Raheem! I couldn't wait on you to get myself together," I lied.

"Oh shit, I'm sorry! You just had a nigga worried. Doe would have my fucking head if I fuck up again," Raheem confessed.

"I won't tell if you won't tell Raheem."

I folded my arms across my chest because my attitude was completely fucked up now and Q had me in my feelings. I wasn't sure if I made the right decision anymore. Judging by the way that Q slammed the door in my face, I knew that door was closed regardless of how I felt. When I got home, I headed straight to the bathroom and took a long hot shower. Not only did Q piss me off, but he turned me on and I needed to clean myself up.

Over the next few days, Q had my head all the way gone. I was back to being a bitch to Moochie and Doe, and I sat cooped up in the house because I was doubting myself and my future with Doe. As frustrated as I was, I had to pull myself out of that shit because it was the fourth of July and we threw a cookout every year. It was noon and Doe slipped out of bed around seven o'clock to handle some business while I continued to snore. However, the chefs and servers started to arrive, and I had to get up to ensure that everything came together.

"Bestieeeeeeeeeeeeeee!" Moochie called out into the foyer and I walked over to the banister.

"Bring your loud ass upstairs," I yelled back.

"What's been up with your moody ass? Are you pregnant or some shit? One minute you're cool and the next minute you back to ignoring a bitch," Moochie sat down on the bed.

"I'm not pregnant. I have been battling with some internal feelings," I informed her.

"Like what?" Moochie inquired.

"Nothing that I can tell you. I don't need you running the shit back to your cousin," I stuck my tongue out.

"I would never," Moochie grasped her chest.

"You're still earning my trust back," I quipped.

"Whatever, let me get cute. I'm trying to see which one of the trap niggas coming home with Moochie tonight," Moochie joked before she grabbed her outfit and left the room.

By four o'clock, the party was in full swing. The interior and exterior of our house was covered by people. The majority of the people in attendance were on Doe's payroll, but there were also a few friends sprinkled into the mix. Moochie and I were seated by the bar throwing back shots when Meechie walked over and interrupted us.

"Jayla and Moochie, this is one of our new members of the team, Q. Q, these two are the BFF's from hell," Meechie was talking shit behind us before we could even turn around.

I whipped my head around and my breath was caught in my chest. I couldn't believe this shit! Prince Charming himself was standing there in the flesh. I was ready to piss in my pants at that moment. Q was looking just as sexy as he did the day I ran into his rock hard abs at the mall. Although Q had my panties soaking wet, I was terrified that Q would disclose our history since he clearly had no idea that I was his boss's woman.

"I don't feel so good y'all. I think I had too much to drink," I announced and hopped up from my stool and sprinted towards the house.

8
Q

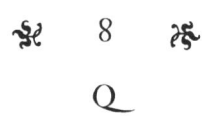

The moment my eyes connected with Jayla, I had mixed emotions. I was ecstatic that I decided to put some effort into getting dressed this morning, so she could see what she was missing out on; but on the other hand, I was pissed that she was here because that meant her man was one of these niggas on the team. Judging by the way she rushed off, she wasn't trying to get caught up. I only caught a quick glimpse of her perfect ass in the coral bathing suit with the white coverall before her friend was in my face.

"Ewwww, I know you have to be new around here because I definitely haven't seen your fine ass around," Moochie ran her index finger across my chest.

"Man Moochie, you get on my fucking nerves!" Meechie walked off.

"I'm the female version of you twin!" Moochie called out behind Meechie.

"Oh that's your twin for real huh? I can see it now," I noted.

"Yeah that's my twin, but I look way better than him," Moochie stood and twirled around.

Moochie was just as fine as Jayla. With her caramel skin toned, a perfect pair of slanted eyes, and one deep dimple in her left cheek,

Moochie was a little too forward for me, but I decided to entertain her since Jayla wanted to be stuck on a fuck nigga.

"You damn right. What you drinking on?"

"Goose," Moochie cooed before reclaiming her seat at the bar.

"I'll take a shot of Henny," I informed the bartender, taking the seat that Jayla previously sat in.

"So when did you join the team and what do you do?" Moochie questioned after I threw my shot back.

"Damn, you the feds?" I questioned.

"Nigga, don't ever play me. Anything my brother knows, I too will know, don't even worry about it. Where your bitch at? That's all that really matters to me," Moochie took another sip from her cup.

"Single as fuck. Which one of these niggas you belong to? I don't want to have to lay nobody down in the middle of the party," I stated.

"I'm not a piece of property, I don't belong to anybody. Y'all niggas play too many games for me. When I said I'm the female version of my brother, I meant that in every way possible," Moochie licked her lips.

I sat with Moochie flirting for the next few minutes. I was enjoying the conversation with Moochie, but I couldn't lie; Jayla was on my mind heavy. I knew I was on her mind too when I glanced up and saw her standing in the window, staring at us. I couldn't miss her coral and white bathing suit even halfway across the yard. I quickly looked away, so Jayla wouldn't know she was spotted. I gripped Moochie's hand and placed a gentle kiss on her knuckles for added effects. I didn't know what the fuck Moochie was talking about from the moment I saw Jayla in the window; I was only putting on a show. I glanced back up to the window to see if Jayla was still there and her arms were folded across her chest; and if I was close enough to see her face, I'm sure she was pissed. The moment Jayla realized she was caught, she quickly walked off and I couldn't help but laugh inside.

"What was that for?" Moochie questioned, taking me away from my own thoughts.

"You got a nigga acting different already," I lied, causing Moochie to grin.

Moochie and I spent the next hour of the cookout in the backyard talking while Moochie continued to drink and eat. Just when our conversation was really getting interesting, Jayla marched over.

"Moochie, I need you inside," Jayla grabbed Moochie's arm and stormed off.

I shook my head and finally allowed a slight chuckle to escape before I went to grab some food off of the grill.

"Young nigga Q!" Doe called out to me after I stuffed the last piece of ribs in my mouth.

"Wassup Doe?" I greeted my OG with a dap and a hug. "I have been wondering when I would see you at your own party."

"Man, when you throwing the party, you gotta make sure shit is running smoothly. I'm glad that you've taken us up on our offer. Even if it is only for the next year, I respect that. Stack your cake up and go back to school and never look back at this street shit," Doe preached.

"That's the plan," I confirmed.

"Now we are going to get you setup with a few niggas we need knocked asap. I got soft and let a few niggas slide while I was going through some shit in my home life. Now niggas think shit sweet," Doe informed me.

"Names and addresses is all I need," I replied.

"My nigga!" Doe dapped me up before he went to mingle with a few other guests at the party.

I scanned the backyard for Jayla and Moochie, but I came up empty, so I went and chopped it up with Meechie on the business tip for the remainder of the party. Once the backyard was cleared, the last few people in attendance stood around the kitchen stuffing the to-go cartons with leftovers.

"You think you can give me a ride home?" Moochie tapped me on the shoulder.

"I got you," I closed my to-go carton just as Jayla walked into the kitchen.

I grabbed Moochie's hand and headed for the door.

"Bye Jayla, I'll call you tomorrow," Moochie slurred.

"I know you're not driving," Jayla fussed.

"Nah, I got her," I replied without breaking our stride.

I know I was being a petty ass nigga. But I didn't give a fuck. As hard as I was, Jayla hurt my lil feelings when she ghosted me. I ain't never had nobody do that to me. By the time we pulled into Moochie's driveway, she was sound asleep, emitting light snores with her head against the window. I gently tapped her shoulder a few times before she actually stirred, but she didn't wake up. I moved Moochie's head from the window and walked around to the passenger seat and opened the door. It started to drizzle and the light sprinkles finally woke Moochie up.

"Shit," Moochie wiped her eyes.

"Let me help you inside beautiful, I got a few moves to make," I coerced.

Moochie had way too much to drink and the sleep didn't seem to help her as she slowly stood from the car. I helped Moochie to the door and made sure she was safely in her bed before I turned to exit the home. On the way out, I stopped to pick up a picture with Jayla in it. I picked up the photo and there Jayla was next to Moochie and Meechie with Doe's arm draped across her shoulder. I couldn't believe this shit! Jayla was Doe's girl.

9

JAYLA

I walked around the house for the remainder of the party with a screwed up face after seeing Q kiss Moochie's hand. Yes, I was in a relationship and ghosted him, but still, there were plenty of other bitches at the party that he could have pushed up on. I know he heard Meechie say we were BFF's; the nigga was trying to get under my skin, and the shit worked.

"Why you been looking like that all day?" Doe questioned, slipping into bed after his shower.

"It was hot as fuck and you had a million and one people over here," I answered.

Really, I didn't give a damn about the heat or the people in attendance, but I obviously had to come up with something because Doe had asked me that question at least ten times today.

"Let me help you take off the edge," Doe pulled the covers back and pulled up my dress.

Before I could stop him, Doe's tongue was already pressed up against my love button. I guess that's what I get for sleeping with no panties on. As good as it felt, I was standing firm in my assertion; Doe needed to take his nasty ass to the clinic first and he had yet to do so.

"Stop Doe," I gently nudged at his head, but he refused to part ways with my clit so I let him keep going.

After reaching my little piece of ecstasy, Doe attempted to reposition himself between my legs.

"Fuck no!" I used all of the force in my body to push Doe off of me.

"What's up bae?" Doe looked on with pleading eyes.

"No! I told you to go get checked and you haven't."

"But I just gave you head Jayla, stop playing."

"I'm not playing with you and you are starting to make me feel like you got something to hide," I rolled my neck.

"Man, stop playing with me Jayla," Doe tugged at my thighs.

"I'm not playing with you Doe! I don't know what you were doing while I was away. I also don't know what that stripper bitch might have so go get checked before you try to swing your dick this way," I pulled my dress down and hopped out of the bed.

"How long do you expect me to go without sex and not cheat?"

Doe stepped in front of me with a serious expression on his face. I couldn't even express myself properly because I was that damn mad. I had to breathe and count to ten.

"See that's exactly the problem! You had the audacity to fix your lips to ask me some shit like that! Get the fuck out! Go fuck another bitch. I don't care anymore," I fumed.

"Yes, you do care Jayla, so don't talk like that. I wasn't trying to be like that either. I was just trying to prove a point. I'm not about to go anywhere," Doe wrapped his arms around me.

"Get off of me Doe! I don't care where you sleep, but you not sleeping next to me," I announced.

"Well you must be leaving the room this time. I'm sick of that shit, all I wanted to do was lay up with my woman and I can't do that. If you wanna sleep alone, pick a room," Doe laid in bed and turned on the TV.

I proceeded to shower again since my juices where everywhere and I retreated to the guest bedroom on the first floor.

"You ain't said nothing but a word," I mumbled before slamming the bedroom door on my way out.

When I woke up the next morning, I got myself together and

headed to the nail shop for a fill in. As I sat in the chair, I connected my airpods to my iPhone and called Moochie.

"Hey bitch," Moochie still sounded all groggy and shit.

"See, you going to get enough of trying to keep up with the fellas while they are drinking. You do know you're half their size right?" I joked.

"You called to pester me when you know I'm fucked up?" Moochie whined. "What you want girl?"

"I saw you all boo'd up with that new face yesterday. You ain't even notice I disappeared for awhile," I noted.

"Yes lawd, Q is so fine," Moochie bubbled. "He even called to check on me this morning. I was so glad he was there to take my drunk ass home. He looks a little younger than I usually like them, but he'll do. He kissed me on my knuckle and shit instead of trying to tongue me down like these niggas usually do. I might have to keep him around."

Hearing Moochie all giddy over Q had me beyond pissed.

"You fucked him?" I blurted out and my nail technician looked up at me, reminding me where I was.

"Damn bitch, I am not a hoe, but I'm going to fuck him as soon as I get the chance. Probably today or maybe tomorrow, I haven't decided yet," Moochie burst out laughing. "More than likely tonight though, I'm going to hit him so we can link up."

"Oh shit, Doe is beeping in, let me call you back," I lied before disconnecting the call.

As bad as I wanted to be honest with Moochie about Q being the man I spent time with while I was away, I knew she would run it back to Doe because they dealt with each other on a business tip. I still didn't know exactly what Q's role was within the organization, but I'm sure Moochie got more out of him than me since Q always made it seem like he was getting a regular nine to five.

Once my nails were on point, I headed out of the nail shop. I struggled with my next move. I wanted to call Q, but then again, I really shouldn't. But I decided to anyways. I located his contact information and dialed the number; it rang once before Q picked up.

"Yo, who this?" Q answered the phone and just the sound of his voice had me burning up inside.

"It's Jayla. I just..."

"You got a nigga and I'm respecting that, don't hit this line no more," Q cut me off and barked before he disconnected the call.

I pressed his contact again to call him right back just to find out this nigga blocked me! I whipped my car out of the parking spot and called Moochie as I headed over to her house. Although I couldn't disclose why I was so pissed, I still needed her at this moment.

"Wassup?"

"Are you still home? I'm having a fucked up morning and I need to relax," I explained.

"I'm home and I'm up and feeling refreshed. Come on over bestie."

The nail salon was only ten minutes away from Moochie's house, and she was outside digging through her car when I pulled up.

"Who brought you your car?" I questioned.

"Doe and Meechie just left here a few minutes ago. That's why I'm up. He told me y'all got into it again last night. I'm sick of y'all asses," Moochie grabbed her bag and headed towards the door. "I don't want to sit around listening to that shit all day."

"I'm sick of us too shit. Sometimes I really wonder did I make the right decision coming home."

"I can't call it bestie. I can't sit here and talk bad about my cousin, all I can say is you need to do what's best for you," Moochie mentioned. "Now cheer up hoe and take a shot," Moochie pulled out a bottle of vodka and two shot glasses.

Moochie and I sat around talking shit for the next hour until I decided I felt a little better and wanted to head back home.

"So what does Q do?" I blurted out once we made it to the door.

"Meechie told me he's a hitta. Why? Let me find out you trying to get my cousin knocked."

"Shut up girl," I hugged Moochie before I left her home.

The drinks had me feeling so good as I pulled out of Moochie's driveway that I thought I spotted Q's car at the four way stop sign. When I pulled up to the stop sign, I realized it really was Q's car. If he really thought he was about to mess around with Moochie, he had me fucked all the way up! I slammed on the brakes directly in front of Q's car and hopped out. Q was fumbling around with something inside of his car and didn't notice me approaching until I was banging on his passenger window.

"What the fuck Jay?" Q looked up.

"Open this fucking door!" I hollered, not caring about how the scene looked.

Q quickly hit the locks and tossed a duffle bag on the backseat.

"What the hell you doing, Jayla? I got some shit going on. I need you to get gone."

"No Q, what the hell are you doing over here? You really trying to fuck my best friend?" I quizzed.

"Ain't nobody thinking about that girl!" Q bellowed.

"Don't raise your voice at me Q!"

"Jay, get the fuck out of my car! I'm in the middle of some shit."

"No! If you don't care about her, then why did you check on her this morning? Why are you headed over to her house?"

"I checked on her because she was fucked up last night. I had to walk her to her bed, she could barely make it out of the car. I have compassion, no matter who a mufucka is. Plus, I'm in the area to handle business that you are fucking up, I ain't here to see Moochie," Q explained.

"Whatever!"

"Why the fuck you care anyways? You forgot to mention to me that you was engaged to the nigga when I was dropping dick off in ya," Q retorted, pointing at the rock on my finger. "I'm trying to keep my job. Your secret is safe with me shorty. Now move around... I hope you find a nigga who won't have you out here looking like a hoe. I told you I got business to handle."

Q leaned over and opened my door just as another car pulled up blaring its horn at my car stopped in the middle of the road.

"Fuck you Q!" I mumbled before exiting his vehicle.

10

DOE

Jayla had been hell on wheels since she got home. But after our last spat, I decided to give in and go get tested like she requested. A nigga didn't have any symptoms, so I figured I was clean. I just hated doctors, no matter what the reason was. I never even had a STD test done in my life, so I had to Google the shit. From what I could find, the fastest and most incognito way for me to have it done was to go through Lapcorp; they allowed me to make the payment online so I didn't have to be in the lobby telling all of my business.

After giving a blood and urine sample, I was in and out within twenty minutes, and now I just had to play the waiting game. I wished I could have paid for one day results, but I had to settle for one to two days. When I walked back into the house, Jayla was sitting in the dining room eating lunch.

"Oh you finally went and got tested?" Jayla noted, taking a look at my bandage on my arm from having blood drawn.

"I did for you Jayla," I confirmed.

"You did for yourself nigga. I went to the gynecologist, I know I'm clean, and that's why I ain't touching you."

"Jayla, when are you going to cut all this damn attitude?"

"When you start acting like the man you say you want to be," Jayla stood up from the table and threw her plate in the trash. "I will give it to you though, going to get checked is the first step," Jayla mentioned before walking into the guest bedroom and shutting the door.

Since I let that stupid ass shit slip out of my mouth on the fourth of July, Jayla had been giving me the silent treatment like never before. She ignored me around the house unless it was something dire, which only happened one time over the last week. Then today would make a second time.

While Jayla was still in a mood, I decided to head to the spot and handle a few things. After making sure the numbers were right and everybody was on point, Meechie and I headed out.

"Slide with us Doe, Jayla ain't paying yo ass no mind anyways," Meechie yelled across the parking lot.

"Where y'all boys going?"

"To grab some food and drinks," Meechie informed me.

"Alright, I'm going to ride with you. A nigga tired as fuck," I sauntered over to his car.

"Where we going?"

"Shit, I'm following Beanie," Meechie pulled out of the parking lot.

The moment we pulled up to King of Diamonds, I knew I should have driven my damn self.

"Nigga, you said y'all were grabbing food. You know I told Jayla I wasn't going to the strip clubs no more."

"Man, shut your cry baby ass up," Meechie laughed before he stepped out of the car.

"Give me your keys, I'm going home... you can catch a ride with one of these niggas. I'm already in the dog house."

"Nigga, Jayla won't know unless you tell her. Just don't get drunk enough where you can't feel the bih pull your dick out and you good money," Meechie coerced.

I still followed his ass inside, although I knew I should have gone home. After a few drinks, I was feeling lovely, but Jayla was on my mind heavy. I knew she would fuck me up if she knew where I was, so I was seated in a corner away from my niggas with all of the cameras out.

"Long time no see," Cheeky planted her chocolate ass in my lap.

Cheeky and I used to kick it heavy until I decided to propose to Jayla. Cheeky was probably the only bitch I fucked on the side who knew how to play her position. She never opened her mouth and Jayla never found out about her, so I still dropped her cash here and there off of the strength of that.

"My ass shouldn't be up in here right now," I noted.

"Well you here and you ain't asked me to get up yet and your dick is standing at attention," Cheeky smiled before she stuck her hands down my basketball shorts.

As bad as I wanted to make Cheeky stop, I couldn't. I hadn't fucked nothing since Jayla went missing. Cheeky's soft hands caressing my tool were the closest I got to getting some in weeks. I was trying to hold strong for Jayla, but I couldn't any more.

"Let's go back to your crib," I whispered in Cheeky's ear before she hopped up and went to get changed.

After letting Cheeky catch all of this pent up frustrations, I quickly showered, redressed, and had her drop me off at my car, so I could head back home. This is why I fucked with Cheeky; she didn't want Jayla's position as long as she was taken care of.

I snuck back in the house around three o'clock and I went to bed. When I woke up the next morning, I slipped back out before Jayla was up. Although that nut felt good last night, the guilt was consuming me. I sat back in my office after running some numbers at the spot thinking of creative ways to get back into Jayla's good graces. My phone rang, pulling me out of my thoughts.

"Hello," I answered for the unknown number.

"Hello, my name is Carol with the Labcorp. May I please speak with Derrick Jones?

"This is Derrick," I sat up in my seat, anticipating the results of my STD test.

"I am happy to report that all of your tests came back negative," Carol explained, and I could finally breathe a sigh of relief.

"Thank you Ms. Carol," I sang into the phone. "Can I come in and pick up some type of paperwork to prove that I'm clean?"

"Yes, just come in and request your medical records," Carol

informed me. "Is there anything else that I can do for you today Mr. Jones?"

"No ma'am. Have a great day," I spoke and disconnected the call.

I was shitting bricks the last seventy-two hours while I waited for those test results to come back. Now, I just prayed that Jayla would give in and give me some because jacking my dick wasn't an option after last night.

KNOCK! KNOCK! KNOCK!

"Who is it?" I sat up at my desk and yelled through the door.

"Q."

"Wassup my boy?" I questioned, opening the door for Q.

"Shit, I can't call it," Q walked in and dapped me up.

"Ya ass need to call something. We had Tone at the crib with a bitch waiting for you to play grim reaper and you ain't make shit happen. What happened man?"

"I was there, shit I was putting the scope on the rifle. Then I... uh... I had some domestic shit pop off while I was in position and waiting. I couldn't get the shot off fast enough once I got rid of her," Q explained.

"I know all about those domestic squabbles. I fucked up more than a few bags behind my woman," I laughed.

"I hear ya," Q noted.

"But we are going to get another shot. You better believe that," I acknowledged.

"You can bet that," Q dapped me up before I hit him off with his paper for his other work, making Loc and Bleezy disappear.

Once Q left the office, I headed to the hospital to pick up my paperwork, so I could take my good news home to Jayla. The moment I walked through the door, I wished I would have stayed my ass at the spot.

"So you was in the strip club?" Jayla questioned. "I hope you had fun."

Jayla slammed the door to the guest bedroom once she was inside. I should have brought my dumb ass home.

11
JAYLA

The moment I got word that Doe was up to the bullshit, hanging out in strip clubs again, I was pissed. As much as I loved Doe, I just couldn't understand why he wouldn't change. I stayed at Moochie's house for the next few days while I tried to get a grip on my life. Today, I decided to get out and do some retail therapy then headed over to The Cheesecake Factory to enjoy dinner alone. I threw back a few drinks as I thought about my life. My parents loved Doe, granted they didn't know about the issues in our relationship, but they loved his spirit and the fact that he took good care of me. Hell, everybody loved to scream how we were couple goals and I couldn't understand how; our relationship was anything but peachy since his public mishap with the stripper. As much as I loved Doe, I was sick of his inability to treat me the way that I deserved to be treated.

Money didn't solve all problems and I was walking proof of that. Sitting at the table alone with my nails and hair to perfection, sporting jewels and designer was cool. But deep down inside, all I could think about was how happy I was with my short time with Q. Q made me realize that I was forcing shit with Doe and missing out on life. I finished my last long island and waved down the waiter.

"May I have the check please?" I questioned once she approached the table

"I already got it," Q took the seat across from me.

"That's correct ma'am. He already covered your bill and a really good tip," the waitress beamed before she walked off.

"Why did you do that? I already got a nigga remember? You told me not to hit your line anymore and damn near shoved me out of your car. Just leave me the hell alone Q," I stood to leave, but Q pulled me back into his lap.

"I couldn't handle you the way that you deserved to be handled because I was in the middle of taking care of some business. I didn't want you in the vicinity when shit went down. You was moving so fast that you didn't notice the rifle I had to shove down by my legs. You were too busy running that mouth," Q flicked my lips.

"So it's true that you're one of the hittas?" I questioned.

"Look, we really can't be doing this shit out in the open. We're right around the corner from my place, let's go talk. My food should be up by now," Q placed me back on my feet, and I couldn't help but smile and follow his lead.

Q grabbed his to go order on the way out and I followed him to his house. Although Q handed me my ass the other day, just the few moments I spent with him had already lifted my spirits. I couldn't really explain it, but in that moment, I didn't care to figure it out either. When we got back to Q's house, he grabbed a pair of shot glasses and sat down at the table with his food, and I took the seat next to him while he ate.

"So are you ready to answer my question now?" I questioned after throwing back a shot.

"What was your question again?"

"Are you a hitta?" I rolled my eyes because I knew good and well he remembered my question. "You always made it seem like you were getting a legit job while you took a break from school."

"Yeah, I'm a hitta. We both were telling half truths. What I do as a side hustle ain't something I'm proud of or go around talking about with everybody, you feel me?"

"I get it, I just…"

"You just what?" Q cut me off. "You lay next to a deadly nigga every night. What I do is nothing compared to him."

"First of all, I don't lay next to him at night. I sleep in the guest bedroom. But what I was going to say was I liked you more because I thought you weren't in the game. I've been with a nigga in the game for a long time and I know what comes along with that."

"Well, I ain't in this shit forever. I don't have a mean jump shot and can't run a football, so I had to put myself through college. I'm putting myself in the position so I don't have to be involved in this shit. As long as you eating off of drug money, you ain't no different."

"I guess you're right."

"Not guess, I am right. Now why you was in there looking all sad and shit?"

"I'm sure you probably already know," I retorted.

"Nah, I don't, so tell me what's up?"

"You didn't go to the strip club with the rest of the fellas a week back?"

"Nah, I don't do strip clubs. When they asked me to slide, I declined and took my ass home."

"A man after my heart," I cooed, feeling the effects of the liquor.

"Let me guess, your man was up in the strip club, so now you're in your feelings?"

"Not only was he there, but he was ducked off with a stripper in his lap looking all comfortable and shit according to one of my cousins," I mentioned.

"Well, that's what you like right?" Q closed his to go carton and went to place it on the stove.

"Damn, what happened to the Q I used to know? He was so sweet and attentive," I stood and followed Q back into the kitchen to sit my shot glass in the sink. I already had three long islands today and I still needed to make it home.

"You lost him when you chose the nigga that doesn't realize what he has in front of him. I ain't hating or nothing, I'm just saying. I hope you putting yourself in position just in case shit don't work out. I know you lied before and told me that you were living off of investments. Stop capping, you living off of Doe, and that's your man, so I get it.

Just make sure you always have something to fall back on," Q spoke, walking back over to where I was standing.

"I'm going to. But I don't want to dwell on my problems."

"We are not going to dwell on them, we are going to talk about some shit though. So take a seat," Q instructed as he sat on the couch and I sat next to him. "What did you go to school for?"

"My bachelor's degree is in psychology, and I used to run a nonprofit that helped families transition from homelessness, but we lost our funding a few years ago, so we had to close down. I haven't done anything since then," I expressed.

"Well why that nigga ain't give you the money to keep the shit running?"

"He wasn't at the top like he is now," I explained.

"He is now though," Q quipped.

"I guess I just hadn't thought about it."

"You have been living comfortably off of him so you haven't thought about it? What if that nigga die tomorrow or get sent to the pen? You going to be straight?" Q quizzed.

I took a moment to think about Q's questions because I never really thought that far ahead. I came over here to feel better, but Q was hitting me with some real shit that had my mind going into overdrive now.

"Your silence just gave you away. Shit, you like to joke about my age, but you need to take a few lessons from me," Q continued.

Keeping all of my feelings and thoughts bottled up inside since I couldn't vent to Moochie about Q finally got to me as I broke down crying.

"Calm down Jayla, why you crying? I'm just trying to drop some jewels on you," Q pulled me in for a hug and placed a kiss on my forehead. "My mama was you, and when my pops was sent to prison, she didn't have shit to fall back on and that money don't last forever."

"I know. I've just had to keep all of my feelings bottled up since I left the hotel. My best friend is Doe's cousin, so I can't talk about my feelings about you with her or anybody for that matter."

"Oh, so you do have feelings for a nigga?" Q inquired, wiping my tears away.

"Yes, I have feelings for you," I confessed. "I have been struggling to figure out if I made the right decision or not."

I looked up at Q through my tears and although he didn't respond, I could see in his eyes and his actions that he still had feelings for me too. I seized the moment and pressed my lips against Q's, and we indulged in a passionate kiss for a few moments until Q pulled away.

"We can't be doing this shit, Jayla. I shouldn't have even approached you at the restaurant."

"Oh, so you don't have feelings for me?" I vexed.

"It ain't that Jayla, but you are engaged to the nigga I make moves for. We both know we don't want those kinds of problems. I ain't scared of that nigga or no shit like that. Don't get that fucked up, but come on Jayla, you can't act dumb like this shit ain't wrong, plus one of us would have to die if this shit got out. Which one would you choose: me or him? You don't even have to answer that, it's a rhetorical question. You already made your decision clear, so I'm not about to do this shit with you," Q stood up.

"If you ain't scared of him, then don't think about him right now," I stood to my feet and sucked on Q's neck.

I knew everything Q said was true, but I couldn't help my feelings. I knew how sensitive Q's neck was, so the moment I sucked and twirled my tongue across it, he wouldn't be able to turn me down. Plus, I needed this. I hadn't had sex since the day I left Q, and all I could think about was getting another taste of him. Giving in to my gesture, Q picked me up and led me to the bedroom and we went at it for at least an hour.

Between the liquor and passionate makeup sex, we passed out and I woke up the next morning to a plethora of missed calls and texts from everybody, even my parents. The last text from Moochie let me know why my phone turned into a hotline.

Moochie: I have been calling your ass all night. If I don't hear from you soon I'm going to have to tell Doe you're missing because I'm worried as fuck.

"Fuck!" I hopped out of the bed.

"What's wrong bae?" Q stirred awake.

"I should have told Moochie I wasn't coming home. I have been staying with Moochie and she got worried and told Doe that I didn't come back to her place last night. Now my mama, daddy, and everybody calling and looking for me," I informed Q as I gathered my things.

I threw my shorts back on just as Q's phone rang and he held his finger up to his lips, signaling for me to be quiet.

"Wassup Meechie?" Q answered the phone. "Alright, I'll come help. Y'all know where she might hang out at? Or any of her friends besides Moochie?" Q paused for a moment. "Just give me a few to get dressed and I'll hit the streets," Q disconnected the call.

"What did he say?"

"They got everybody out here looking for your little ass. He just asked me to come help," Q informed me. "I'm about to hit the shower. You better hit somebody line before they find your ass over here."

Once I was dressed, I grabbed my purse off of the couch and headed back into Q's bedroom to grab my phone. Upon entering the room, my phone began to ring; it was Moochie, so I quickly grabbed the phone off of the bed to answer it.

"Hello," I answered the phone, attempting to sound groggy like I just woke up.

"Jayla? Is this Jayla? Why are you answering Q's phone?"

I froze up and quickly hung up the phone.

"Fuck! Fuck! Fuck!" I yelled as the iPhone rang in my hand again.

My mind was moving so fast that I didn't realize I only saw Moochie's name flash across the screen and not her contact picture. I marched into the bathroom with the ringing phone in hand.

"Why the fuck is Moochie still calling you? I thought you said you weren't checking for her!" I exclaimed.

"I ain't," Q yelled over the water.

"Get out of the damn shower and answer this. I just accidentally answered your phone for Moochie!" I exclaimed.

"How the fuck you do that?" Q turned the water off.

"I thought it was my phone," I paused. "Just answer the shit Q! She already thinks it was me who answered and this is her third time calling. Tell her it was another bitch or something."

"Man, I knew I should have sent ya ass home last night," Q

complained right before I accepted the call and put it on speaker so I could hear too.

"Wassup Moochie?"

"Don't what's up me, was that Jayla who just answered your phone?"

"Jayla? Nah Moochie, that was my girl Cam and now she on my ass so I gotta go."

"My bad, I'm probably just tripping because I'm worried as fuck," Moochie sighed. "After you handle your bitch, come meet me so we can go look for Jayla. She didn't come home last night and nobody has heard from her since she left my house around three o'clock yesterday. It's already noon... it's almost been twenty-four hours since anybody last heard from her and this is really not like her, so we are losing it."

"Let me handle shit with my girl and then I'll hit you," Q disconnected the call.

"I think she bought it," I was finally able to breathe again.

"Alright, now get home Jayla," Q growled.

"Why do you sound like that?" I questioned.

"If you don't know, then don't worry about it," Q stepped out of the shower and grabbed my arm before he pulled me to the front door, still naked and soaking wet.

"Get back to your life, Jayla," Q opened the door and damn near threw me out of it.

"Fuck you Q!" I yelled outside before I stormed towards my car.

"Nah, fucking me is exactly what you ain't *ever* doing again," Q snickered and slammed the door.

I pulled off and rushed to Moochie's house breaking, all traffic laws. Halfway there, I silently cursed myself, realizing I left my phone at Q's house. When I pulled up to Moochie's house, her car was no longer in the driveway. Since I didn't have a phone or a way to contact anyone, I went inside and took a shower. This would be the perfect cover; I'd sit here like I had no idea what was going on and say I lost my phone. After showering and changing into a pair of leggings and a t-shirt, I went to the kitchen and made a bowl of cereal before I planted myself on the couch to watch old episodes of *Prison Break* on Netflix. After a few hours past and Moochie didn't return home, I headed to Sprint to grab a new phone to really drive my excuse home.

12

Q

After I pushed Jayla's ass out, I got dressed and rolled a blunt to ease my mind. Jayla had me all the way fucked up if she thought I was going to play side nigga to Doe. I shouldn't even be considering dealing with Jayla, but I was. However, the shit was going to have to be on my terms and not hers. Jayla had my nerves so fucked up that I ended up blowing two blunts and taking a shot of Hennessy to drown out my thoughts. Just as I closed my eyes, my phone rang.

"Hello," I answered for Meechie.

"What's up bro? You was supposed to be hitting the streets bro, where you at?"

"Oh shit, my bad. I'm headed that way right now," I hopped up from the couch. "Moochie asked me to roll with her so let me see where she at."

"Moochie is at the spot, just get ya ass up here."

I grabbed my keys off of the counter and placed a call to Jayla's phone. Jayla left here almost two hours ago, so there was no reason she shouldn't have popped up or called them. Just as my hand touched the door, I heard Jayla's phone ringing in my bedroom.

"Fuck," I mumbled to myself.

I went to retrieve Jayla's phone and powered it off and threw it in the trunk of my car before I took off. On my way to the spot, I was fuming. Jayla had more games than a little bit. Even if she did leave her phone at my crib, she still should have popped up on her people by now. As I walked down the hallways, I could hear Moochie, Doe, and Meechie talking, so I stopped walking to hear what they were saying.

"Some shit ain't right. Jayla has run off on me a few times, but she always tells her parents where she is. She ain't popped up yet and she ain't in jail. After y'all run by all of the hospitals in the area, it's a green light on them niggas, they gotta know something! I shouldn't have let her go stay with yo ass," Doe vented.

"Don't try to put this shit on me!" Moochie exploded. "If you would keep your dick in your pants, she wouldn't have been staying at my house. You cut all of them other bitches off, but you still fucking the stripper bitch Cheeky! Jayla's cousin said y'all was all cozy and shit! I told you to leave Jayla alone if you ain't going to change."

"I ain't even wanna go to the strip club," Doe argued. "This nigga said everybody was going to eat, so I hopped in the car with him and then this fool pulls up to King of Diamonds."

"So what, you could have caught an Uber home."

"I might have tricked you into pulling up, but I ain't tell you to leave with the stripper though," Meechie blurted out, and I heard a loud slap.

"What you hit me for?" Doe based.

"Meechie just told on your dumb ass. You left with that bitch! I swear Doe," Moochie chastised Doe before she stormed out of the office, and I took a few steps to appear as if I was walking instead of eavesdropping.

"You ain't going to tell Jayla when we find her are you?" Doe came rushing behind Moochie. "I promise, that's my last fuck up. I'm going to marry Jayla and do right, I swear. Just don't run this shit back to her or we ain't going to make it."

"Fuck you Doe! All you need to do is focus on finding her," Moochie rolled her eyes. "About damn time!" Moochie screeched in my direction, walking towards me.

"Yeah man, you were supposed to be on your way two hours ago," Doe added.

"Moochie got me into some shit after my girl answered the phone when she called," I noted.

"Nigga, listen to me and listen to me good. Do right by your woman if you love her," Doe somberly expressed but that shit didn't move me. He wasn't shit and I knew it.

"Well I don't care about your feelings," Moochie spat at Doe before she turned to me. "I damn sure don't give a fuck about your bitch or her feelings. Ya ass told me you were single on the fourth of July anyways, but I don't even care about all of that. I just need to find my bestie so come on," Moochie stormed out of the backdoor.

I trailed behind Moochie with my anger growing by the second because I knew Jayla's ass was alright, and I could have been doing other shit with my time. Moochie drove me all over Miami, and when I say everybody was out looking for Jayla, *everybody* was out looking for her. We even ran into a few of the fellas as we stopped at the last hospital within the city limits to see if she was there.

"I'm about to call the police. Doe wants to keep the police out of it, but I don't give a fuck what he has to say at this point," Moochie pulled out her phone.

"Maybe you should call Doe and talk to him first," I placed my hand over Moochie's phone. "We are by your crib, call him, and we can stop by your place so you can have a moment to breathe."

"Okay Q," Moochie smiled. "Your girl better hold on to you tight."

"Yeah, about that. I'm trying to make shit work with my girl, so we can't cross those lines," I expressed.

"A faithful man I see, I can respect that. But the moment she acts up, Mama Moochie will be right here," Moochie flirted as she pulled into the driveway.

I instantly became more pissed when I saw that Jayla's car was not there. The only reason I tried to get Moochie to go home was because I thought Jayla was there. Moochie hopped out of the car and called Doe as we approached the door. After Doe heard Moochie's plan to call the police, they started bickering, so I decided to step outside. When I opened the door, I came face to face with Jayla.

"What the fuck you doing here?" Jayla vexed. "Moochie calling your phone and now you at her crib looking all comfortable and shit. I'm about to fuck you up."

"I had to pretend to look for your simple ass because you didn't reach out to anybody. Moochie is about to call the police because she's losing her damn mind," I gritted. "Come get your phone out of my trunk and make yourself known before you get somebody hurt."

"Toss that phone somewhere, I just bought a new one," Jayla held up a bag from Sprint. "When I get this phone programmed, you better have unblocked my number. Oh, and make that the last time you treat me the way you treated me today, Q! Now move!" Jayla pushed past me and entered the house.

Jayla was lucky that we were at Moochie's house or I would have bent her over right there. I couldn't lie; the way she switched her attitude and tried to put me in my place had me turned on. Jayla needed to just stop playing and let me wife her; at this point, I was ready to risk it all for her.

"JAYLAAAAAA!" Moochie screeched, rushing to Jayla and wrapping her arms around her neck. "I was worried sick about you! I just had to curse Doe out because he wouldn't let me call the police and your ass is just fine!"

"Yeah, I'm good. Why y'all tripping?" Jayla played dumb.

"Bitch, we have been calling, texting, and looking for you all day! Where the fuck have you been? You didn't leave the house wearing this yesterday, and I know you haven't been home because your parents are over there sitting, just in case you went there."

"I have been here all day. I went to see my friend Tammy in Lauderdale yesterday and I crashed there. I came back around noon and waited for you to come home. I just grabbed me another phone from Sprint because I lost my other one, so relax," Jayla lied her ass off, and I made a mental note to check her ass about how good she was at it.

"Alright, call everybody and let them know what's up. These boys burning the city and was ready to start questioning the other side about Jayla's whereabouts," I announced.

Jayla just didn't know that she was about to start a war and that's why Doe didn't want to get the police involved. Once everyone knew that Jayla was safe, I headed to the bar to drink. A nigga couldn't get his thoughts together. My heart was playing tug of war with my mind. My mind said stop fucking with Jayla but my heart was telling me she could be the one if she wakes up.

13

DOE

I was pacing the floor in the office after snapping on Moochie for trying to call the police. This shit here was truly a wake-up call for me. I don't know what I would do if I lost her, especially behind some street shit. Just as Meechie and I were headed out, Moochie called me and my world brightened up again when she informed me that Jayla was safe and at her place. After Moochie ran down the situation to me over the phone, I rushed over to her house because I still needed to lay eyes on her after such an emotional day.

"Jayla, you had us worried as fuck!" I barged into Moochie's house.

"Were you worried about me when you were up in the strip club?" Jayla hissed.

"Come on Jayla, don't be like that, you don't understand how I have been feeling all day. I been fucked up thinking that something might have happened to you," I confessed. "Please come home Jayla. Even if it is to sleep in the guest bedroom, I will give you all of the space that you need. I just want to be the one to ensure that your safe."

"Then tell me the truth Doe, have you cheated on me since I moved back home?" Jayla looked me into my eyes, searching for the answers I damn sure wasn't about to give.

"No, I haven't. I was only at the strip club because my stupid ass hopped in the car with Meechie," I quickly cut my eyes at Moochie. "Yes, I was dead wrong for staying. I should have Ubered home. But I promise to never make that mistake again. Now please come home baby."

"I'm not convinced," Jayla quipped.

"Alright, well if you want to stay here, I understand. I'm willing to give you all of the space you need. But Raheem needs to take you ANYWHERE you need to go. Do you understand me?" I questioned.

"Why? I only take him if I don't feel like driving or if I'm drinking. I don't need a babysitter," Jayla protested.

"Jayla, we are in the middle of some street shit. I was losing my mind thinking that you got caught up in the middle," I divulged.

"Okay Doe," Jayla conceded.

"Why couldn't you have at least called or text anybody to let us know where you were and that you were good?"

"I just needed some space Doe, damn," Jayla barked. "You keep fucking up and we only getting older. I'm really starting to wonder if this shit is even worth it."

"Don't talk like that Jayla," I pulled Jayla up from the couch and wrapped her up in my arms.

I used my finger to lift Jayla's face so she could look me in my eyes. I could tell by her facial expression that she wasn't ready to talk and wanted me to leave. I placed a kiss on her forehead and reluctantly headed for the door.

"I'm going to right all of my wrongs, Jayla," I announced before I exited Moochie's place.

On my way home, I stopped at Chick-fil-a to grab something to eat. My mind was still in overdrive trying to figure out how I could make shit right with Jayla. When I pulled into my driveway, Cheeky was calling me, which wasn't like her. I thought about answering just in case she really needed something, but after what I just went through with Jayla, I needed to stay on the straight and narrow. I didn't need her convincing me to come over. Jayla just didn't understand; she was making it hard as fuck for a nigga while she withheld sex.

After a good night of sleep, I woke up the next morning and it hit me exactly what I needed to do. I needed to move up the wedding. I grabbed my phone off of the dresser and called Draya.

"Hello Mr. Jones," Draya's angelic voice sang into the phone.

"Hello Draya, I think we are having some big changes, and I would like to come in and talk about them. Do you have anytime today?"

"Can you come in at two o'clock?"

"I'll be there," I confirmed before I disconnected the call.

After showering and getting myself together for the day, I made a few moves to check on our operation before my meeting with Draya. As I sat in the lobby, I texted Jayla to let her know I was thinking about her. I needed to get my home in order fast before I lost it all.

Me: Good morning beautiful. I promise from this day forward I'm a new man. I just wanted to let you know that I'm thinking about you. I love you Jayla. I am going to pick you up for dinner later tonight.

Jayla: Okay.

Me: Damn, no I love you too?

Jayla: Nah nigga, you have to earn that back.

Me: I will, trust me.

"Mr. Jones, where is the future Mrs. Jones?" Draya greeted me.

"This is all a surprise to her. I want to move up the wedding to prove to her exactly how committed I am to this relationship," I explained.

"Come into my office, so I can pull out the plans that we had so far and discuss dates," Draya turned on her heels and walked down the hallway and into her office. "Since we hadn't paid any deposits yet, we won't have any problems with changing the date. How soon are you looking to move things up?"

"I was thinking about a date next month. I really want to make this a surprise for Jayla. Our dating anniversary is on October 19th. I was thinking about that date if we can move that quick."

"Wow, I mean we can move that fast, but it's going to cost you. That date is only three weeks away, and we are going to have to drop some cash to become the priority and skip to the front of the list for things like flowers, cake, DJ's, and photographers. The only place that I see us having an issue is the venue. The type of venue that Jayla had in mind is usually booked months, hell sometimes, a year in advance," Draya divulged.

"I ain't sweating that. My crib is as big as they come, and we throw parties there all of the time. I'm sure we can accommodate the wedding. We are probably going to cut down on the guest list just a little since we won't be giving people much notice. I'm only telling Jayla's parents and my mama. Everybody else will be kept in the dark so nobody ruins it until I'm ready, and whoever can make it, can make it," I explained.

"Well that sounds like a plan Mr. Jones. I'm going to start calling around. We can still make decisions based off of everything Jayla went over during our consultation. The only thing I would highly recommend that you have Jayla do is help with cake tasting," Draya advised.

"I can do that," I confirmed.

"Okay, here is her information. I'm sending her a text now," Draya handed me the card while texting. "She is great, she did my wedding cake and we have a good relationship, so I can get her to squeeze you guys in for a small fee. Call her today and try to get in there today if you can. But no later than tomorrow and we will have ourselves a wedding on October 19th," Draya celebrated.

"Thank you so much. I'm going to see the misses now, but I am in the dog house, so I probably won't be able to get her there today... but I definitely will get her in there tomorrow."

"No later than tomorrow Mr. Jones," Draya ordered. "Now I need to sit down and get the ball rolling on everything else. Ohhhh, I just love your style Mr. Jones."

Draya's last statement caused me to smile and made me feel like I was doing the right thing. I just prayed that Jayla would be just as impressed. After leaving Draya's office, I texted Jayla and told her I was on my way to pick her up. When I arrived, Jayla was dressed and ready to go. My eyes roamed Jayla's perfect body in the yellow dress that provided the perfect contrast with her mocha skin tone. Jayla's perfect smile was present as I was the perfect gentleman, opening her door and closing it once she was seated in the car. As I maneuvered through traffic, I gripped Jayla's hand tightly, and for the first time in a long time, she seemed to be in a good mood while in my presence.

"I love you Jayla," I pulled her hand up to my lips and placed a kiss on it.

"I love you too Doe," Jayla sighed. "I only wished I didn't love you."

Jayla's words cut me deep, so I was silent the rest of the ride there. I still was going to give this shit my all though. I walked around to Jayla's side of the car and opened the door. Moochie gave me the tip to take her to the Cheesecake Factory so here we were. I held Jayla's hand as we walked inside and pulled out the chair for her before we were seated. Halfway into dinner, I started getting the ball rolling with my plans.

"I made an appointment for tomorrow to go cake tasting at this spot Draya recommended. Is that cool?"

"That's cool with me," Jayla replied.

"I also want you guys to go look at dresses next week and get those measurements and shit done, so we can get that part out of the way early; and then we will only have the small stuff to worry about after that."

"Look at you, really taking charge," Jayla noted.

"I told you, you're looking at a new man," I proudly stated.

"I sure hope so. I'm going to have Moochie as my maid of honor and Tammy as my bridesmaid and that's about it. So I'm sure we can get in there next week."

"That's perfect. I'll just have Meechie as my best man and Beanie as my other groomsmen to match your two. So are you ready to come home?"

"I'm sick of staying on Moochie's couch, so I'm coming home to MY guest bedroom. I still need space and time before we can act like everything is all good again."

"Whatever you want and need Jayla," I complied.

After grabbing the check, I spotted Cheeky walking into the restaurant, and I couldn't believe my luck. I held my breath as Cheeky and one of her friends from the club walked past our table. Miami was too damn small at this point. I kept my eyes glued on Jayla to avoid any attention until my phone pinged.

Cheeky: I been calling you all day. I was calling you for a reason. You know I'm not the type of bitch to sweat you. But

you better meet me near the bathrooms right now or I'll forget how to play my position.

"Let me run to the bathroom before she comes back with my card," I announced and quickly hopped up from the table.

"Okay," Jayla replied, pulling out her phone.

I rushed towards the bathroom on pins and needles to see what Cheeky wanted. I said a silent prayer that she wouldn't be on no dumb shit tonight.

"Don't look so stressed. I'll be quick," Cheeky voiced once I approached her.

"What's up Cheeky? I been handling business all day."

"Whatever nigga... I ain't your bitch, you don't have to lie to me. I called you because I'm pregnant," Cheeky blurted out.

"What the fuck is that supposed to mean?" I got defensive as I felt my last glimmer of hope with Jayla dwindle.

"What do you think dumb ass? It's yours. Look, I'm not trying to fuck up your happy home. Just give me the money for the abortion. That's the least you could do."

"Here," I pulled out a wad of cash from my pocket and peeled off ten hundred dollar bills and passed them to Cheeky. "That should be enough for the abortion and then some. From this day forward, I'm making things work with my girl. I know I said this before, but I mean it this time. I'm getting married soon so shit between us is over. If you ever need anything, you can always hit Meechie and he'll make sure you straight."

"Thanks. I appreciate it, now was that so hard? A simple reply to my text or a returned phone call could have prevented this little meeting," Cheeky walked off.

I went into the bathroom to splash some water on my face before I returned to Jayla. When I walked back into the dining area, Cheeky was standing at the table next to Jayla. I rushed over as fast as I could and caught the tail end of the conversation.

"Yeah girl, what's your Facebook name? I can send you her contact information through messenger. I know she can get you right for your wedding," Cheeky smiled, and I quickly took the seat and attempted to calm my nerves.

"Look for *Jayla Jones*, thank you for the plug," Jayla replied.

Cheeky clicked around on her phone before she announced that she sent the message and proceeded to her table.

"Her hair is cute right? I think that would be perfect for our wedding day, so I had to stop her," Jayla informed me.

"It's alright. I think you'd look better with your natural hair straightened," I stated my opinion.

"Well I'm getting that hair. I never wear bundles, let me live for just that day."

"I already told you, whatever you want. Are you ready to go?"

"Yep," Jayla gathered her belongings and we headed out of the restaurant.

As soon as we got home, Jayla hit the shower and kept to her word, retreating to the guest bedroom. The shit crushed me a little, but I was willing to play her game. Once I was in the room alone, I texted Cheeky.

Me: Please don't be on no bullshit.

Cheeky: Your bitch grabbed my arm and asked me about my hair. I can't help it that she wanna be like me. Ain't nobody going to say shit to the girl. Now you told me we're done. So we're done!

14

JAYLA

Since I returned home, things were really on the up and up, so I hadn't bothered Q since I saw him at Moochie's house. To my surprise, he hadn't hit me either. I was cool with it though. It looked like it was time to really give this thing a real shot and stop creeping behind Doe's back. The only reason I was even considering sticking around after the strip club drama was because I had fucked up too.

At Doe's request, Tammy, Moochie, and my mother were out dress shopping, and I was actually excited about our wedding again. The dress that I had my eyes on was still available and I stood in front of the floor length mirror in the dressing room; and even I had to admit, I was stunning it this dress. The long sleeved lace mermaid gown was everything. The moment I stepped out of the dressing room, all conversation ceased as everyone took in my appearance.

"This is the one for sure," my mother broke the silence and walked in my direction with tear filled eyes. "My baby is getting married."

"Awwwww stop that sappy stuff Ms. Jennifer," Moochie replied.

"You guys like it?" I questioned.

"We love it!" Tammy added in.

"It looks great," Maria, the designer, added in. "We will just need to make a few minor alterations."

"I'm going to take it," I announced.

"They have a few coral dresses that we like too. As soon as you're out of that dress, we can try them on for you," Tammy informed me.

After Maria pinned the dress up for alterations, we switched positions. Tammy and Moochie went to try on the dresses they picked out while I helped my mother browse for a dress as well. Once Tammy and Moochie exited the dressing room, I knew those were the dresses for them. After finding the perfect dresses, we headed back to my mother's house, and she made us a nice dinner.

"So what did you and Jayla get into that had her so busy she couldn't even call her mother last weekend?" I heard my mother question Tammy while I was in the kitchen.

"Huh? We weren't together last weekend," Tammy responded.

"You wasn't?" Moochie whipped her head around in Tammy's direction.

"Ummmmm, I don't remember chile," Tammy caught on and tried to cover for me, but she was doing a trash job. The stares that were coming my way from Moochie and my mother let me know they weren't convinced.

"Mama, why you so dang nosy? Let me be great when I want to. Now y'all help me get this menu and seating arrangements together so I can go home. I'm tired. I never knew you had to plan this shit out this far in advance. Draya asked for this back by the end of the week, and it's already Wednesday."

"Ummmm hmmm girl," Moochie cut her eyes at me.

"So Tammy and Moochie, when are you ladies going to settle down?" my mother questioned, obviously to the can of worms she just opened.

"Ms. Jennifer, I don't have time to let a nigga add stress in my life and send me to an early grave."

"Marriage ain't easy, it's going to be hard. But when your ass is old and alone, then what?"

"Alright Mrs. Jennifer, get her together," Tammy chided, snapping her fingers, and Moochie's attitude instantly changed and started giving Tammy dirty looks.

Tammy was a good friend I met in college, and she never got along with Moochie. That coupled with the fact that Tammy lived a little further out is why I never thought to tell Tammy about the lie I placed her in. Tammy was a successful realtor. We checked on each other from time to time, and we would end up talking for hours and it was like we never missed a beat.

"So what about you Tammy? Do you have anyone special in your life?" My mother continued her line of questioning.

"Not yet Ms. Jennifer, but I'm hoping that God sends me a man to sweep me off of my feet next. I ain't none of Moochie, I can't be hoeing when I'm old and grey."

"Alright, alright," I rushed over with the makeshift seating chart I created to stop those two from coming to blows. "Ma look this over, I think I have the people who don't get along separated."

My mother grabbed the legal sized piece of paper and scanned the names on the seating chart.

"While she does that, Moochie you need to be thinking about who we should separate from y'all family."

"Chile, our family all gets along for the most part. Just don't sit Uncle Ronny next to Aunty Melody. You know their divorce is fresh, and Aunty Melody has really been hitting the bottle."

"Are you sure that's all? I don't need anybody turning up at my wedding. You know your family is a little more than just ratchet, those mufuckas lethal," I articulated.

"Girl, they wouldn't mess up Doe's wedding. They know he will handle their asses in the middle of the ceremony."

We spent the next hour finalizing the menu and seating arrangements. I hugged and kissed Tammy goodbye before she headed back home, and I instantly wished that I didn't ride over with Moochie this morning. But Doe was still on me about not moving alone, but he made an exception today since Moochie knew how to handle a gun.

"You think you getting off that easy?" Moochie questioned as we cruised down the interstate.

"What?" I played dumb.

"Where the hell were you when we were looking for you? Tammy ain't got nobody fooled. You wasn't in Lauderdale with her."

"Yes, I was," I argued.

"Why are you lying to me Jayla? The only reason I'm all in your shit is because I could have sworn it was your voice I heard answer Q's phone that day you were missing. You fucking that boy?"

"No Moochie! Is you crazy? Why would you even say that?" I yelped in my defense. "Do I look that dumb?"

"Bitch ion know, I can't call it right now," Moochie momentarily took her eyes away from the road to glance at me.

"So where were you?"

"I was in Lauderdale, but I wasn't with Tammy," I blurted out the first lie that came to my mind. "I went to look at places out there because at that time, I was really considering leaving Doe and starting over there."

"Why didn't you just say that if that's really what you were doing? You know I don't give a damn about whether or not you leave Doe."

"I don't know Moochie, you are my best friend and I love you to death, but Doe is still your cousin. Blood will always trump our friendship."

"When it comes to you and Doe, I'm on the side of what's right. If you want to leave that nigga, leave him sis."

"We are in a good space now Moochie, but if I do decided to leave him, I promise not to leave you in the dark next time."

"Okay Jayla," Moochie replied.

When we pulled up to my house, Meechie and Doe were standing outside with Q and a few other fellas from the team.

"What they got going on?" Moochie questioned, stepping out of the car.

"I don't know."

"Hey y'all," I provided a generic greeting and attempted to keep walking.

"Come here Jayla," Doe called out, stopping me before I could get too far.

"Shit getting crazy out here. So from this day forward, Raheem is to be with you at all times. If you need to go somewhere and you can't reach him or me, hit Q or Meechie. I don't want you to argue with me either. It's not permanent, it's temporary. We just have to tie up a few loose ends, and until they are handled, we are on high alert and your safety is a top priority."

"Okay Doe," I answered as my eyes met with Q's momentarily, and I swear his ass got finer every time I saw him.

"What's up? What's going on?" Moochie questioned.

"That nigga Tone figured out we tried to hit him and he knows too much about us. So until he gets got, you need to keep your head on a swivel too," Meechie answered.

"You know I ain't your average bitch. I stay ready," Moochie patted her purse. "Y'all was all out here rapping, I thought it was something bigger than that."

"Nah, that's it," Doe responded.

"Well I'm out," Moochie threw up the peace sign and walked back to her car.

I headed inside and left the men to do their thing. The next day while Doe was out working, Raheem took me to the hair salon and sat in the car while I tried out some bundles for the first time. I wanted to make sure the shit would really work with my face before my wedding day. After my hair was washed and blow dried, in walked the same cute chocolate girl that gave me the recommendation.

"Bianca, can you squeeze me in for a touch up please?" she pleaded with the stylist.

"I got you since you brought me a new customer," Bianca motioned towards me.

"I knew your face looked familiar. Jayla right?"

"Yes," I extended my hand.

"I'm Cheeky," Cheeky pushed my hand away. "I'm a hugger chile," Cheeky announced before she bent down and wrapped her arms around me.

"You got in here fast didn't you?"

"Yes, I'm trying to get cute for the weekend," I answered.

"Well Bianca will do it for you. So what kind of hair are you getting?" Cheeky sat in the empty chair next to us as Bianca started braiding my hair down.

"The same hair that you have. It's my first time having a sew-in. My man likes me natural, but I'm trying something different," I bragged.

"Is that right? Most niggas don't understand the natural hair struggles."

"Mine does, his mother has always been natural so that's all he knows."

"Owwwwwww girl, look at that rock," Cheeky leaned over and lifted my hand up.

"Yes, I must admit, my baby did his thing when he picked this out," I admitted.

"He sure did. You better hold on to him tight. I saw his fine ass the other night. I'm sure he has hoes beating down his door. You better lock him in," Cheeky voiced.

"He better get his shit right and lock me in, I'm the prize," I expressed confidently.

"Well I can't wait until I find my prince charming to lock me down," Cheeky laughed.

"You should come to my wedding. There will be plenty of fellas there who are single. You better grab you one. I probably can put you down with a friend," I offered.

"You know what… that sounds nice. Maybe I will come to y'all wedding. I mean, I am the reason that your hair will be slayed on your big day."

We sat in the salon kicking shit for the remainder of my time in the chair. Just as Bianca started to put on my closure, my phone rang. I pulled it out to see Q's name flashing across the screen. I ignored him the first time, but when he called a second time, I decided to answer.

"Hello," I answered.

"We need to link up asap. Where you at?"

"Why do we need to link up?" I inquired.

"Just meet me somewhere real quick," Q requested.

"We ain't talked in weeks and now you're calling and demanding that I meet you somewhere. Shit don't work like that."

"If it wasn't serious, I wouldn't be calling."

"Well how am I supposed to get up with you anyways? You know

Raheem takes me everywhere because of whatever the fuck y'all got going on. I can't ask Raheem to drop me off to you," I rolled my eyes.

"That's why I asked your hard headed ass to give me your location."

"I'm sending it to you now," I informed Q. "Do you have a back door I can use?" I questioned Bianca.

"Yeah girl."

"Make sure you come around back," I directed Q and disconnected the call.

Q was right on time after Bianca ran her curling wand through the last piece of hair. I paid Bianca for her services, exchanged phone numbers with Cheeky, and headed out of the backdoor.

15

Q

Jayla was almost unrecognizable with her hair in this style. I was used to the braids or the messy bun, but Jayla was beautiful no matter how she wore her hair. I planned to have this conversation right here, but the moment Jayla flashed her smile my way, I pulled away from the hair salon and headed back to my place.

"Where are we going Q? I didn't expect to leave with you."

"Just sit back and relax."

The moment the door to my house was closed, Jayla started with her attitude, only turning me on more.

"Why the fuck you brought me over here?"

"Lower your voice and watch ya mouth when you talk to me. I'm the one with the questions, what did you tell Moochie?"

"What you mean?" I questioned.

"Moochie asked me to come to the shop to help her with some shit, which was already out of the ordinary because she's in charge of the money and nothing else. After I helped her perform a few menial tasks that any of the other niggas already there could have handled, she started asking me questions about you," I divulged.

"I didn't say shit to her. We were kicking it with my friend Tammy, who I lied and said I was with, and she mentioned that I wasn't with her. Moochie asked me last night were we fucking, but I assured her that wasn't the case. Maybe she just wanted to see if you had a different answer. If she really thought something and was going to say something to Doe, she would have and he would have killed me already."

"You sure Jayla? That's why I wanted to see you. I want to make sure you're straight."

"I'm good, now you need to take me back before Raheem figures out I'm gone."

"What if I ain't ready to let you leave?" I asked.

"Too bad, if that's all you wanted to talk about, I gotta go," Jayla sassed, heading for the door.

"Nah, you got me fucked up," I pulled Jayla back into the living room.

"Q, what's wrong with you?"

"Since I laid eyes on you, I realized how much I missed you. Plus you all fine and shit," I expressed before mashing my lips up against her.

Jayla's hands invaded my basketball shorts as my hands roamed her entire body. Our tongues danced off of each other, which was intoxicating. I hadn't been fucking with Jayla because I was trying to move on and let her do her thing; and clearly, she was doing the same because she hadn't reached out to me either. However, it felt like we hadn't missed a beat in that moment.

"Wait... stop Q," Jayla pulled away. "We can't do this no more. That's why I haven't bothered you since that day at Moochie's house."

"When I was spitting them same lines, you didn't give a damn so I don't either," I lifted Jayla off of her feet and carried her into the bedroom and tossed her on the bed. I grabbed a condom from the nightstand and walked back over to the bed.

"But we shouldn't," Jayla weakly protested.

"I know, that's why you sitting her soaking wet, barely putting up a fight," I dropped my boxers and slid the condom on before I pounced on Jayla.

Since I knew Jayla had to go, we made it a quickie; although I wanted to lay up in there all night.

"You going to get us killed," Jayla noted after wiping herself off in the bathroom and throwing back on her clothes. "I requested an Uber and he is already outside. I need to hurry back because I think the hair salon closes at seven and it's already 7:30. You over there looking all drained and shit, so I didn't want to rush you to get me back."

"Nah, you didn't drain me enough," I pulled Jayla into my lap and placed another sloppy kiss on her. "You should've let me end things when I tried to end things. I still don't think you and that nigga going to make it... he's going to show his true colors. I just hope you not fucking him."

"How the hell are you going to ask me some shit like that?" Jayla quipped.

"Well that gives me my answer. We can end things for sure now. I ain't trying to fuck behind that nigga."

"If you must know, we haven't been intimate since I moved out of Moochie's house. I've only been home for a few days, and with everything going on, he isn't home as much as he usually is. I barely see him," Jayla confessed, which was music to my ears.

"If you give him some pussy, lose my number," I advised Jayla.

"Bye Q! How about you just lose my number off of GP," Jayla hissed before she walked out of the door.

After overhearing Doe's confession of fucking the stripper, I knew it was only a matter of time before he was caught up again. I was willing to wait until that shit unfolded. As bad as I wanted to tell Jayla, I couldn't because I felt like she would have trouble believing that type of information coming from me because we both knew I wanted her.

I let Jayla leave without protesting because a nigga was tired. I was working around the clock trying to put an end to our problems with Tone, but we kept coming up empty since Doe wanted to be discreet.

16

DOE

"What the fuck you mean you don't know where she at?" I scolded Raheem.

"I just asked the ladies from the shop and they said she left an hour ago. But I was watching the door like a hawk. I never saw her come out," Raheem expressed. "I even went to all of the business in the plaza, and I called her phone and she didn't answer. I'm just trying to do the right thing and let you know asap just in case something did happen."

"Get ya dumb as over here right now!"

After I disconnected the call with Raheem, I called Jayla's phone twice and she didn't answer. I paced the floor feeling like déjà vu all over again. Just as I was getting riled up, Raheem called me back.

"My bad boss. She was here the entire time," Raheem confirmed, and I was slightly relived but that was the last straw for this irresponsible ass nigga.

"After you take Jayla home, make sure this is your next stop!" I demanded.

I sat back in the chair and rolled a blunt to ease my mind. We were in the middle of some real beef shit and we couldn't afford no slip ups. Not even for a moment. Clearly, Raheem was too incompetent to comprehend that. After I finished the blunt, my phone pinged and I had an incoming picture message from Cheeky. There was a picture of Jayla in the hair salon, and the photo was zoomed in on her engagement ring.

Cheeky: I don't know Doe. I ain't know you was rolling in the dough like that. I might need more than a stack and the offer to look out when I need some shit for me to keep your secret.

Me: Man Cheeky what kinda shit you on? I've always looked out for you and this how you wanna play it?

Cheeky: I'm just saying. All I got was a few handbags. Meanwhile, she has a driver/babysitter that she has to sneak away from. Plus that big ass rock had to have cost you a grip. You always made yourself seem small time to me. All I ever got was a few bags and a stack here and there. She up in here Fendi down! I'm sure she would love to know I fucked her nigga every Friday night for the past year up until y'all got engaged.

I sat back and weighed my options and decided not to engage with Cheeky. After blowing another blunt, my phone pinged again and I almost didn't want to pick the shit up. But the moment I saw the screenshot from Cheeky with a typed text message addressed to Jayla's phone number, I quickly called her.

"What the fuck you want Cheeky?" I massaged my temple.

"I just thought I might send your bitch a text since her nigga, my baby daddy, wanna ignore me. She all bragging about you in the shop and shit. Meanwhile, homegirl don't even know how dirty of a nigga you really are."

"Cheeky, just tell me what you want and I got it," I conceded.

"I'm about to be real with you. After seeing how your bitch living, me and my baby might need the same treatment," Cheeky suggested.

"I thought you got an abortion?"

"I was scheduled to go in on Monday, but now, I think this baby might be my meal ticket sent straight from God," Cheeky cackled.

"You think this shit funny Cheeky?"

"Nah, I don't think it's funny. But I'm dead ass serious. How much money do I think this secret is worth is what I'm trying to figure out."

"Cheeky, just have the abortion and I will pay you whatever you want."

"I'll hit you when I have a figure, and I won't have the procedure done until I have every red cent," Cheeky hung up on me.

My anxiety was at an all time high now. Every time I tried to get my life on the right track, this type of shit happens. I couldn't win for shit with these hoes. I walked over to the shelves on the opposite side of the room and grabbed the Hennessy to throw back a few shots. I was on shot number two when Raheem finally showed his face.

"So explain to me how the fuck you call me and tell me you don't know where Jayla is then a few minutes later she was there the entire time? How that shit work?" I cut right to it before Raheem could get comfortable. The only reason I wasn't breaking my foot off in his ass was out of respect for his big brother Beanie. If me and Beanie didn't go way back, all bets would be off with this incompetent muthafucka.

"She was in the shop getting her hair done while I sat in the car, and when I saw them closing up, Jayla didn't come out. I walked up and asked the lady who owned the shop, and she said Jayla left an hour ago," Raheem explained.

"I'm still not understanding nigga! Why the fuck wasn't you in the shop with her?"

"I wasn't about to sit in there and listen to a bunch of bitches gossip for hours," Raheem asserted.

"We have a snake in the camp who can hit us at any moment. I pay you a nice chunk of change to make sure that my woman is safe, but you can't do that. You sitting up here telling me you didn't want to hear gossip, so you stayed outside where you couldn't see what the fuck was going on in there! Now explain one more thing to me, how did you find her? Another bitch at the shop said some shit about Jayla sneaking off."

"She just walked out of the BBQ joint a few spaces down," Raheem claimed. "She said she went to get something to eat."

"Well I don't give a fuck what happened. Your ass is done in this operation. Take the L and move around," I opened the door.

Raheem's jaw was tight as he clenched his fist. But I was unfazed because I knew the nigga wasn't that damn stupid. Raheem sauntered out of the room looking like he was ready to murder a nigga. I demonstrated how little of a fuck I gave as I slammed the door on his ass. The fact that Raheem couldn't find Jayla, and Cheeky mentioned how she had to sneak away from her driver wasn't sitting well with me. Now, I was questioning a lot of shit, going all the way back to her disappearance a few weeks ago. I grabbed my keys off of my desk and flew out of the office to get some answers from Jayla.

The only thing on my mind was the idea of Jayla fucking around on me. I would lose all of my cool and murder somebody tonight if my suspicions were confirmed. Ain't no way all of this shit was a coincidence; whatever she was up to, I was going to find out tonight! I swerved in the residential area on two wheels trying to make it home. The moment I slowed down at the first set of speed bumps, shots rang out.

RATATATATATATATATATATA!

Before I could react and shoot back, I lost control of my car and ran into the wrought iron fence in front of the house on the corner. Tires squealing could be heard in the distance as I attempted to pry myself from the front seat. My head was throbbing and I could hardly see with all of the blood in my eyes.

"Oh my God! Somebody has been shot!" I heard a woman call out before I lost consciousness.

My eyes flickered open and I was sitting in the back of the ambulance strapped down to the gurney.

"He's regained consciousness," one of the EMT's announced.

"Mr. Jones, can you hear me?"

"Yes," I answered.

"Sit tight. You have a concussion and a gunshot wound to the side of the head. Thankfully, the bullet just grazed you."

"Can you call my fiancé please?" I pleaded. I was in a slight panic because I could only remember back to the phone call I received from Raheem telling me he lost Jayla. Everything else after that was blank.

"I'm sorry, we didn't grab any of your belongings from the scene. The police were logging items in as evidence to try to find out who did this to you."

"I can't remember shit," I expressed.

"Calm down Mr. Jones, you will have all of the answers you need soon and someone from the hospital will get in contact with your fiancé.

I laid back silently cursing myself for getting caught slipping. I thanked God that he didn't allow this nigga to take my life. My mind was drawing a blank about why I was headed home so early and without my team. But I already knew whose finger was on the trigger, and Tone's ass was going to be six feet under as soon as I got to my phone. All bets were off. I didn't give a fuck about the consequences at this point; if them old heads wanted to go to war behind their disloyal ass family member, then that's just what it was. It was on sight and no need to hide after this stunt.

17

Q

"You told me to lose your number remember?" I answered Jayla's phone call.

"You know I was just mad. But I don't want to hold you long. I think my ID, credit cards, and debit cards must have fell out of my purse at your house."

"I didn't see anything left behind," I advised Jayla.

"Can you check the couch?"

"Alright," I lifted myself from the bed and walked into the living room. After pulling out the cushions, Jayla's things were sitting right there. "I got your stuff. I guess you trying to sneak back over here?"

"No, I was hoping that you could bring it to me right quick. Raheem left for the day and Doe doesn't come home until three or four in the morning so you should be fine."

"Alright man, you not getting anymore dick today so just brang ya lil ass outside and grab it real quick," I instructed, grabbing my keys off of the counter.

"I would never fuck you here, I ain't that disrespectful."

"If you say so Jayla, I'll see you in a minute," I disconnected the call.

I gathered Jayla's belongings and headed over to her house. It was a twenty minute drive and I planned to be in and out. When I pulled into their neighborhood, I saw Doe's Range Rover crashed into someone's gate and surrounded by police officers. The truck was riddled with bullets, so I called Jayla as I continued down the street.

"You outside?" Jayla answered the phone.

"Nah, I'm coming down the street. I just saw Doe's car crashed and shot up. You should try to hit him," I informed Jayla.

"Oh my God!" Jayla screamed, and I heard a loud boom followed by loud panting come from Jayla.

My heart was beating inside of my chest because I wasn't sure what the hell was going on. I floored it down the street, hopping over all of the speed bumps.

"AHHHHHHHHH!" Jayla's voice sounded off through my car's bluetooth speakers, and I could hear her breathing hard as she ran through the house.

"Jayla!" I called out.

"Somebody kicked in the front door," Jayla whispered as I pulled into the driveway.

"Lock yourself into a bedroom or bathroom. I'm coming in now."

"I'm in my closet in the master bedroom."

"Stay there," I ordered, hopping out of the car.

I pulled my pistol from my waist and made sure there was one round in the chamber as I silently crept up to the front door, and I could hear Tone ranting throughout the house. I could tell he was on the first floor and I knew Jayla was upstairs, so I was being patient so he wasn't alerted to my presence. Tone might have been on the run, but I knew he wasn't no punk. Look how he went at Doe.

"Where the fuck you at Jayla?!" Tone vexed. "Just come out and make this shit easier for everybody!" Tone continued to move throughout the house, and I was following his voice at every turn until I could find him in the mansion they lived in. "The longer I gotta look for you, the worst I'm going to FUCK YOU UPPPPPPPPPP!"

Once my eyes were locked on Tone maneuvering through the house, I placed the gun on my waist.

"Nigga!" I based before I crept up on Tone and placed him in a firm head lock.

Tone squirmed around, only causing me to tighten my arms around his neck before I drug him back outside. Halfway to the car, Tone's body finally went limp. I dropped Tone's lifeless body on the ground before I pulled out my key fob to pop the trunk. After securely placing Tone's body in the trunk, I rushed back into the house.

"Jayla!" I called out. I would have went to the room and found her to make sure that she was straight, but I didn't know the layout of the house like that.

"Q!" Jayla rushed down the stairs, and I wrapped her up in my arms.

"I handled that nigga. But you should probably get down to the hospital to see about Doe," I instructed her. "I have to make sure I get that nigga's body away from here asap because I'm sure the police will be snooping around here with Doe being shot around the corner."

"Was he okay?" Jayla questioned with concern laced in her voice.

"I don't know, shit happened so fast with you calling and the commotion that I rushed right over here."

Jayla's phone rang and she pulled herself away from me to answer the call.

"Hello," Jayla answered her phone then mouthed that it was the hospital before telling the person on the other end of the phone that she was on her way.

"They took him to Mercy Hospital, I need to get down there," Jayla rushed around the house grabbing her purse and keys.

"Are you okay to drive?" I grabbed Jayla's hand before she made it to the door.

"I'm okay. Plus, I probably shouldn't have you taking me up there," Jayla expressed.

"Alright, just relax and take a deep breath before you get behind that wheel," I kissed Jayla on her forehead.

"I'm good Q," Jayla exited the home. "I need to call Moochie and Meechie," Jayla continued to ramble.

"I'm going to follow you over there since it ain't far just to make sure you're good."

"Okay, I'm leaving now though... they didn't tell me shit so I need to know that he is okay."

The concern lacing Jayla's voice had me hot on the inside. Even though I knew I was being unreasonable, I still couldn't help my feelings. I brushed my feelings off and trailed Jayla until she was safely in the hospital. Then I proceeded to place a call to Meechie.

"Where the fuck you at nigga? Jayla just called me and said Doe is in the hospital. We gotta get that nigga Tone!"

"That's why I'm calling. He's in the trunk right now. I'm headed to get rid of him now."

"For real?! We need this W and it's right on time!" Meechie exclaimed.

"Yeah man, what hospital is Doe at? What they saying?" I quizzed, only halfway giving a fuck.

"He's still breathing, that's pretty much all we know right now. Take care of that and I'll hit you with updates when I have some."

"Bet," I disconnected the call.

18

JAYLA

I was completely shaken up when I walked into the hospital. I can only imagine what would have happened if Q wasn't already on his way over to drop off my belongings. I was grateful for the way everything played out. I watched Doe grab his belongings to be discharged from the hospital after an overnight stay had me in my feelings. When I heard that Doe's car was shot up, I felt my world crumble.

"I love you Jayla," Doe placed a kiss on my cheek.

"I love you too Doe. Don't ever scare me like that again."

"I won't, I talked to Meechie and that nigga is handled. You never have to worry about somebody running up in our house again," Doe assured me. "I'm so glad that you were able to hide out while he ran through the house. Oh, and I forgot to tell you that I fired Raheem yesterday."

"What? Why did you fire Raheem?" I was puzzled.

"The nigga was just doing too much, and when he couldn't find you yesterday, I decided he needed a new profession. With Tone handled, you can come and go as you please, but we will find somebody else to replace Raheem asap."

"Uhhh, okay," I faltered.

"Let me ask you something, where were you yesterday? Shit was a little foggy when I got in last night. But now I can remember everything. Raheem said he couldn't find you, and I heard you left the shop, so I'm going to ask you one time, where the fuck did you sneak off to?" Doe invaded my space.

"You heard I left the shop?" I whipped my head around. "No, I told Raheem that I went to grab some barbecue. I even grabbed your ass some, so I don't appreciate your tone."

"Chill Jayla, I just had to ask for my own peace of mind," Doe softened up and placed a kiss on my cheek. "My mind was thinking some shit I was ready to fuck you up over."

The nurse walked in with a wheelchair and Doe's discharge paperwork.

"Nah, I don't need that. I can walk out, I feel fine," Doe protested.

"I'm sorry sir, it's hospital policy," the nurse retorted.

"Boy, sit down and shut up. I'm ready to go," I pushed Doe towards the wheelchair.

Once we made it back home, Doe passed out due to the lack of sleep. I fell asleep in his arms on the hospital bed. However, Doe sat up all night making calls and complaining about how uncomfortable the bed was. I went to Walgreens to grab some Tylenol for Doe, and I realized that I still didn't have any of my cards or ID. I used the small amount of cash from my purse to purchase the items. On my way out of the drugstore, I called Q's phone.

"Hello," Q's sexy voice greeted me. My panties were instantly soaked and I couldn't help that he had that affect on me.

"Hey Q, I'm sorry to bother you. Are you home? With everything going on last night, you forgot to leave my things."

"I'm at the house. Come through," Q answered before he hung up the phone.

I took the twenty minute drive to Q's house in silence. I had to mentally prepare myself to share the same space with him and not end up having sex. I needed to hurry home to check on Doe. I sat in my car and called Q again in hopes that he would bring my things out to me, but he didn't answer. I got out of the car and walked up to the door. After knocking twice, Q answered the door with his bare chest exposed. I quickly brushed past him and walked into the foyer, making sure that I avoided eye contact the entire time.

"I just need to grab my things and get back home. I left Doe alone and he just got out of the hospital."

"My bad, I had dozed off for a second, your stuff is on the counter," Q walked over and grabbed the few pieces of plastic.

"Thank you for being there for me yesterday Q," I grabbed the cards.

"I'll always have your back Jayla."

"I appreciate that, now I have to go," I rushed back out of the front door before saying bye or giving Q the chance to do the same.

I unlocked my car doors and reached for the door handle when I felt someone approaching me from behind. I quickly turned around to check my surroundings and released a sigh of relief momentarily when I came face to face with Raheem.

"Shit is crazy... Q looks so much different on his ID," Raheem held up the same photo identification card that he confronted me with weeks ago.

"Raheem, what are you doing here?"

"Waiting for you to show up. After Doe fired me, he mentioned that somebody told him you snuck out of the shop. I figured if the nigga, whose ID this belongs to, still lived at this address, you were going to see whoever this nigga was again," Raheem flung the photo ID in my face. "I just didn't expect to see Q open the door. I also didn't think you would show up so soon. I mean, is Doe even out of the hospital yet?"

"I... I... got... gotta go," I attempted to open the car door, but Raheem jumped in front of me.

"Nah, we got some shit to talk about. I never met Q before he got down with the team, and even then, the nigga never got in my car before. Like I previously said, the ID was in my car when you returned it. If y'all want me to keep my mouth shut, I need my salary for the next six months cash by the end of the day tomorrow. Or I'll send this shit to Doe," Q spun his phone around and displayed a picture of Q opening the door for me just a few minutes ago. I stood there in shock.

I couldn't believe my luck over the last 24 hours. "Lil hoe, you hear me?"

My reflexes kicked in and before I knew it, I had slapped Raheem across the face. I could handle the blackmail, but the nigga crossed the line calling me out of my name. I was furious at this point and wasn't thinking clearly. Truly, I needed to comply with Raheem's demands, but he had me fucked up calling me a hoe.

"Bitch!" Raheem grabbed my wrist and twisted my arm around like he was ready to break it off.

"STOP! Get off of me Raheem!" I involuntarily squealed loudly due to the pain Raheem was inflicting on me.

"Fuck that! You was just big bad hitting a nigga right?"

I tried to break myself free by pushing Raheem back into his car.

"Get the fuck off of me!" I screamed at the top of my lungs this time.

PEW! PEW!

"AGHHHHHHHHHHHHH!" I yelled as blood and brain matter splattered all over my face and clothes.

"Shhhhhhh!" Q rushed over with his gun with the silencer attached in hand.

I sobbed uncontrollably as Q pulled out his garage door opener and the door slowly slid up. Q pulled Raheem's body into the garage as I stood there frozen in place, still crying. I had never witnessed no crazy shit like this is in my life.

"Jayla, you causing a fucking scene! Shut the fuck up!" Q barked as he manually closed the garage door before he rushed over to me. Q grabbed my arm and pulled me into the house. "Jayla baby, you gotta calm down," Q softened his tone while rushing to the linen closet to grab a rag. Q rushed back over to my side and gently started cleaning my face. "You gotta calm down and breathe baby."

"You didn't have to kill that boy!" I protested with tears streaming down my face.

"Any nigga who puts his hands on you can catch two to the dome and that's on God. Now you have to get your shit together because I have to clean this mess up myself. I can't call in a cleanup crew because then, I would have to explain killing one of our own," Q informed me.

"What the fuck was he doing here anyways? I never let them niggas know where I lay my head at night."

"When we first met, that car I was driving belonged to Raheem. You must have dropped your ID in there one day because he found it. He tried to give it back to me weeks ago, and I acted like I didn't know who it belonged to. Doe fired him yesterday since he called Doe when he couldn't find me. He came over here because he knew I must have been with you yesterday. But you look so much different in your ID picture that he didn't put two and two together until he saw you open the door. He just knew I was with a nigga named Quinten Phillips at this address."

"The shit is handled now Jayla.... you need to take a quick shower and get cleaned up. I need to clean off my driveway, okay?" Q questioned calmly.

"Okay," I nodded my head in agreement.

I took a quick hot shower at Q's house before I changed into a pair of his basketball shorts and a tank top. I was still shaken up when Q re-entered the house. I couldn't believe that shit had gotten this out of hand between the two of us. After Q got me to calm down, I headed home and Q went to handle Raheem's body. This shit had really become too much.

19
Q

I had to travel out of the area to have Raheem's body disposed of properly and quietly. Otherwise, there would have been too many questions to answer. With shit popping off left and right, I decided to get away for a minute and chose to head back to Tallahassee since it was FAMU's homecoming weekend. My old college roommate Kyle got a job in Tallahassee, so I crashed at his place after attending the football game and hitting the club while I was in town. On my final day, I decided to go chop it up with my advisor. My best bet might really be to get the hell away from Jayla.

With all of the problems Doe and Meechie had encountered over the short amount of time I'd been in town, I had enough money to cover the cost of graduate school. I tossed around the idea of returning to school earlier than expected, so I decided to speak with an advisor while I was here. After sitting in the office, bouncing around questions and scenarios for close to an hour, I had a clear vision on what I planned to do with my life.

When I pulled up to Kyle's apartment building, I spotted Sheena's car in the driveway. She was Kyle's cousin and my ex-girlfriend. I wanted to turn around but all of my shit was there. Sheena and I had a contentious separation. I wanted to move back to Miami for a year and stack my paper, and Sheena wanted me to stay in Tallahassee and get myself into debt for my education. After our last fight about the matter, I took off and moved to Miami before my house was ready. I hadn't spoken to Sheena since then and that's how I ended up meeting Jayla.

I specifically told Kyle not to tell her I was in town. Sheena had called my phone on more than one occasion, but I ended up hanging up on her ass every time because all she wanted to do was bitch about a situation that I had already ended. I sat in the car as I contemplated going in when a text from Kyle came through.

Kyle: Sheena's ass just popped up over here. I ain't invite her.

I looked up from my phone and Sheena stood in the doorway with a slight grin on her face. Sheena had my heart on lock and I truly did plan to marry her after I finished school, but I couldn't do that nagging shit.

"Can we talk?" Sheena gently tapped on my window. I looked up with hesitation written all over my face. "I promise my attitude is in check," Sheena chuckled.

"It better be," I stepped out of the car and leaned against the passenger door. "So what's up?"

"I missed you," Sheena flashed her beautiful smile my way before she leaned into my chest.

"You ain't never act like it. You never called to check on me, only to bitch me out, and put all of your fucked up emotions on me."

"I'm sorry about that. I just didn't want you to leave. I didn't want to do the long distance thing, and I didn't handle myself the correct way."

"I'm glad you know you were handling yourself like a little ass girl. But I apologize as well... I shouldn't have left without saying anything to you, even if you were giving me hell," I confessed.

"I appreciate that. Did you miss me while you were away?"

I stood there quietly for a moment because the truth of the matter was, I hadn't missed Sheena. My mind had been consumed with Jayla since the day I met her. Maybe I needed to do my own thing to get Jayla off of my mind.

"Damn, you didn't miss me just a little bit?"

"I missed how we used to be. I didn't miss all of the arguing and fighting we did the last two months before I left."

"I have grown and learned my lesson, and I miss the hell out of you. So is what Kyle said true? Do you have a girl?"

"It's complicated," I provided a short answer.

"You move on fast don't ya?" Sheena copped an attitude. "To think, I came here thinking you had me on your mind when you decided to make this trip to Tally."

"It just happened Sheena... I didn't mean to fall for somebody else," I confessed, expressing my true feelings. "Honestly, I always thought we would link back up before you got so deep in your feelings and started that crazy shit."

I had love for Sheena, so I wanted to be honest with her and not lead her on in anyway. The defeated look on her face as she lowered her head tugged at my heart strings. I placed my finger under her chin and pulled her head back up.

"It's not that deep. When I say my situation is complicated, I mean just that. I don't know where shit is going, that's why I'm here. I just wanted to clear my mind for a little. It's good to know that you're still as fine as you always were," I flirted with Sheena.

"I'll always be fine. I take care of myself. Since you got a woman and shit, I'm going to slide. I don't want to put you or myself in a complicated situation. I see your man growing, and I ain't trying to turn into your sidechick," Sheena nodded towards my grey sweatpants.

I chuckled at Sheena's keen eye. I was trying to hide the fact that my shit was bricked up. Sheena had the thickest thighs and the fattest ass to match. My eyes were glued to Sheena as she sashayed to her car.

"Are you going to move your car or you just going to keep staring at my ass?" Sheena turned around and cracked a smile.

"Are you going to take me off the block list?" I questioned.

"I think I can do that," Sheena smirked before planting her fat ass in her car.

I snapped out of my trance and brushed Sheena off before I hopped in my car to let her out. Sheena was the one person I was trying to avoid while I was here, but I was sure glad that I ran into her.

The next day, I headed back to Miami to get my life in order. If Jayla wasn't ready to leave that nigga, then I was going to see where things went with Sheena. Sheena had my heart in her pocket at one point and I had hers in mine. She was smart as hell, currently in school to become an OBGYN, and she loved me regardless of my faults or side hustles. More importantly, at least with Sheena, I ain't have to worry about her fucking around with another nigga.

When I got back to town, I checked in with the boys and made sure that shit was still running smoothly. The moment I got home, I requested for Jayla to meet me out of the way so we could talk. I knew we couldn't be out in the open, so I requested that she met me at South Beach Park in Boca Raton. It was an hour drive, but I figured it would be worth it. I grabbed her favorite items from the Cheesecake Factory and sat around waiting for Jayla to show up. My head was spinning as I thought about my next move, but I knew it was the right move. When Jayla pulled up and stepped out of her Mercedes-Benz GLE, the sun glistened off of her skin as the curly hair flowed effortlessly down her back. Jayla now had her ends dyed a different color and the shit only added to her appearance, making her look a lot less innocent than she always did.

"What's all of this?" Jayla approached the picnic table that was covered in a coral table cloth with our food sitting on top of them.

"I just wanted to catch a light lunch with you and talk about a few things. The last time we saw each, other shit was crazy," I expressed.

"Yes, it truly was. I haven't been able to talk about that shit with anybody else, but I have had a few nightmares about it," Jayla's chipper mood changed quickly as she approached the table.

"I'm sorry that shit went down the way that it did. I probably shouldn't have shot him right there in front of you. But seeing him put his hands on you pushed me over the edge quick," I divulged.

"I get it, it was still just a lot. I never seen no shit like that," Jayla advised me.

"If you ever wanna talk, you know you could have called me Jayla," I wrapped my arms around her.

"How? I've been waiting on Doe hand and foot since he got out of the hospital. I had to tell him I was going to see Tammy to get away today."

"Well you're here now. That's all that matters."

I pulled Jayla over to the table, and we enjoyed our meal rather quietly for a change. I was nervous about my proposition, and I'm sure that Jayla's mind was still focused on that bloody scene that unfolded during our last encounter. If Jayla accepted my proposition, she would never have to worry about that type of shit again.

"I have been thinking. I want to stop creeping around," I commented once we finished our meals and were now seated on the sand, watching the waves crash into the sand.

"Well you sure have a funny way of showing that after planning a romantic date for us and shit," Jayla instantly caught an attitude.

"Nah, that didn't come out right," I clarified. "I mean, I want you to leave Doe so we can be together. I'm tired of sneaking around. I'm tired of only having bits and pieces of you. I miss having *all* of you. I'm willing to leave all of this shit behind for you. We can move away to wherever you want, and I will get a job and slow grind going back to school for my masters. All I really want is to be happy with you Jayla, that's all that matters to me. However you want to do it, I'm with it."

"Q, I really think we need to just pump the breaks on this entire thing," Jayla stood from the sand.

"What you mean?" I was perplexed. I truly expected Jayla to tell me to give her some time or something, but I didn't expect her to try to cut me off.

"We have been through a lot in such a short amount of time. If I'm being honest, I have deep feelings for you. I might even love you, but we have to stop this. I already got one person killed behind our shit. We should have stopped fucking around as soon as we found out the role we really played in each other's lives," Jayla walked off as she wiped the sand off of her perfect ass in the jean shorts.

I hopped up and ran Jayla down.

"So you really want to end this?"

"Yes, Q! We are DONE!" Jayla answered with a little too much attitude for me.

"Yeah, yeah, yeah, your nigga ain't fucking you and probably fucking other bitches, so I know you will be back just like last time. Only this time, I'm moving on!"

Jayla slapped the shit out of me before she stormed off to her car. I watched her car swerve out of the parking lot. I shouldn't have said what I said, but Jayla was treating me like I did some shit to her. The drive back to Miami was long and frustrating. I wanted to call Jayla so bad, but I decided to give her what she wanted. Maybe running into Sheena was a sign to really move the hell on.

20
DOE

When Jayla let me know that she was going to be visiting Tammy today, it was perfect. I was sitting in the room calculating the best way to get away from her. Since getting shot last week, I had been communicating with Draya via email to finalize things for the wedding, and we were throwing together a quick party to announce my grand surprise in two days. However, I had one loose end to tie up with Cheeky. This morning, she finally text me and asked for fifty grand to buy her silence; if the bitch wasn't pregnant, I would have just offed her. But if she kept playing with me like she didn't know who the fuck I was, she could be put under.

I drove over to Cheeky's house and pulled into the garage to avoid anyone seeing my car. I gripped the envelope full of large bills off of the front seat and headed inside. Upon entering the house, I could hear Cheeky's freak nasty playlist filling the atmosphere and the aroma of what had to be curry chicken invaded my nostrils.

"Cheeky," I called out into the house.

"Hey baby daddy," Cheeky sang, walking into the living room butt ass naked, wearing only a pair of fuzzy heels.

Cheeky's chocolate body looked good enough to eat as she sashayed over to me. I was pleading with my dick to stand down, but the moment Cheeky dropped to her knees and took my dick into her mouth, I couldn't help but to fuck her face. Cheeky moaned as she sucked and slurped on my dick; light moans escaped my mouth each time my dick bypassed Cheeky's tonsils. I know I said *the last time* would be the *last* time, but this time would *really* be *the last* time. Cheeky laid some of the sloppiest head she ever laid on me and had my toes curling as my dick spit down her throat.

Cheeky stood to her feet and gently massaged her clit as she cupped her left breast with her other hand. I couldn't help but to bend her over with that sight in front of me. After thrusting in and out of Cheeky a few times, I stopped myself. I didn't bring a condom with me because I fully expected to drop this cash on her and slide. I quickly pulled out, not trying to fuck this bitch raw.

"I don't have a condom so I guess it ain't meant to be," I began to pull my pants up.

"I'm already pregnant. Ain't like you can blow me up a second time," Cheeky slowly stood up to face me and stuck her tongue down my throat as she gently caressed my sac. I roughly turned Cheeky back around by her weave and rammed my dick inside of her.

"Ewwww, daddy mad so he trying to get rough," Cheeky cooed as she held onto the wall.

Cheeky was right; a nigga was pissed that I had to drop fifty racks on her scheming ass. I thought Cheeky was the down ass bitch who knew her position, but she proved me dead wrong. The more I thought about the shit, the angrier I got and the harder I pounded in and out of Cheeky. My aggression wasn't phasing Cheeky though; she was throwing that pussy back on me like she had a point to prove. The loud moans that were escaping Cheeky's mouth were filling the entire house... fuck Trey Songz, the neighbors knew Doe's name.

"Come sit me on the stool bae," Cheeky request and I followed her command.

Cheeky sat the stool up against the wall and spread her legs eagle, granting me full access. I dipped inside of Cheeky's honey pot while she held her legs open in a split like she was on stage at the strip club. After a few more thrusts, I pulled out and let my nut go all over

Cheeky, the stool, and the floor. The small amount that was left on my hand, I slapped across Cheeky's face.

"Ewwww, you know I love that freaky shit, baby daddy," Cheeky beamed.

"Stop calling me that shit Cheeky. Get rid of the baby or I swear to God, I'll be getting rid of your ass," I advised Cheeky and threw the envelope full of cash at her.

"I'll just call you *big daddy* then," Cheeky laughed as I walked out of the door.

I flushed it back home to shower before Jayla returned home. This was really going to be my last fuck up. Jayla had my heart and soul from this point forward. Once I was all cleaned up, Draya notified me that she would be sending out the texts and emails to advise everyone of the impromptu gathering at our home. When Jayla returned home, she showered and joined me in the bed.

"I love you Doe," Jayla grinned before she placed a kiss on my lips.

"I love you too Jayla. We are having a big get together on Friday night. I have an announcement to make, so please find you something amazing to wear."

"Okay, what is the announcement?" Jayla pried.

"You will see. I promise it will be worth the wait."

It felt good to hear Jayla say she loved me. I hadn't heard those four special words roll off of the tip of her tongue in a long time. I pulled Jayla back into my arms and we fell asleep in that position. With all of the last minute party tasks to handle, I barely saw home Thursday or Friday. But it was worth it as I watched everything come together. I sent Jayla, Moochie, Tammy, my mother Moni, and Jayla's mother Jennifer to the spa to get manis and pedis, so they would be out of my hair today.

Draya and I walked around the house barking orders for everyone to get things together. We needed the tables and chairs setup in the backyard immediately so the mosquito repellent could be strategically placed next. The catering company was already there setting up the food and the only thing missing was the bartenders.

"Mr. Jones, go get dressed. I talked to the driver and the ladies are on their way back from the spa… it's a forty minute drive and they are already dressed. Guests are already starting to trickle in so we need you on point next," Draya instructed.

"I'm going to take a quick shower and I'll be back down. I haven't seen the bartenders come in yet. Please check on them."

"I got this Mr. Jones, relax a little so you can enjoy this night too. I have everything under control," Draya assured me.

I went upstairs and hopped in the shower. After scrubbing my body down, I hopped out and threw on my clothes as fast as I could. Jayla was wearing a lilac dress, so Draya found me a matching lilac button up that wouldn't be too hot in this Florida sun. Although it was the second week in October, the sun was blazing. After checking myself in the mirror, I had to admit that I looked damn good. My beard was trimmed and not a hair was out of place. After giving myself a pep talk, I walked downstairs to greet all of my party guests.

Meechie and Q were standing by the bar taking shots to the head. Q almost didn't come through and was trying to leave the team earlier than expected, but I was hoping to keep him around until the initial date that he provided. Although we had taken care of Tone, we never knew when the next snake would emerge from the grass and need it's head chopped off.

"Look at this cornball ass nigga wearing purple and shit," Meechie cracked.

"I'm just trying to match my woman's fly tonight. When the fuck are you going to settle down Meechie?"

"Never. I don't want to have to kill a bitch for trying me. I'd rather die alone."

"You sound just like your fucking sister bruh," I noted.

"What about you Q? I expected to meet the woman in your life tonight," I expressed.

"She left me," Q spoke flatly. "I'm working on something else though," Q took a sip from the drink the bartender handed him.

"Mr. Jones, their car just arrived," Draya called across the yard.

I walked up to the makeshift stage that the jazz band was playing on and took my place next to the microphone. I had to think about how happy Jayla made me to get my breathing under control so I could get through my speech. My shit wasn't going to be long and drawn out.

But I wrote the shit all on my own. The ladies spilled into the backyard, and I tapped the microphone to grab everyone's attention.

"Jayla, can you come up here for me baby?" I called out over the microphone, stopping Jayla and her girls before they could make it to the bar.

Jayla smiled meekly before approaching the stage. Draya grabbed her hand and helped her up the small set of stairs in her stilettos.

"What is this?" Jayla whispered to me.

"Jayla, I love you with everything in me. We have had one hell of a year, and I love and appreciate you for holding me down. So much so, that I don't want to wait another ten months to make you my wife," I announced. "So Jayla, will you marry me next Saturday, October 19th?"

I bent down on one knee and pulled out a new ring. It was bigger and better than the one she was currently sporting, and more importantly, it was one that I found on a saved folder on her MacBook after she left me.

"Yes!" Jayla beamed, and I slid the ring on her finger.

On cue, a helicopter started swirling around the house with a banner that read *#JoiningTheJoneses October 19, 2019*. Everyone in the crowd cheered us on as I tongued Jayla down and gripped her ass in the middle of the stage.

"Now let's eat so I can have my fiancé to myself!" I yelled over the mic before I tongued Jayla down again.

I felt like I really made the right move the way Jayla walked around with that huge grin on her face. My mission for the rest of my life was to make her happy and to make sure that she wore that same beautiful smile more than she ever wore a frown. After a few hours of laughing, dancing, and eating, everyone departed the home but not before grabbing their formal wedding invitations.

21

JAYLA

I truly couldn't believe Doe had put in all of this work for our wedding. Initially, I was on cloud nine after Doe made the announcement. However, when I woke up this morning, I was truly in a panic just thinking about how we were going to get everything done in time. But the moment Draya and Doe sat me down and ran through everything over brunch this morning, my mind was at ease again. Doe had really been a sneaky devil, but for once, it was in a good way.

After brunch with Doe, I went to Bianca's shop to pick up the bundles I paid for via cash app this morning. I wanted them in my hand so there was no confusion on my big day, that was just six days away now. With my bundles secured in my passenger seat, I headed home.

I had to pass Q's neighborhood on the drive. I wanted to keep driving, but I really wanted to check on him. After walking off the stage with Doe, I caught a glimpse of Q, who was clearly hurt before he left the party. Five minutes later, I was pulling up to Q's house. I sat in the car for a few minutes before I stepped out. I focused on my pumps clicking against the pavement as I approached the front door. I knocked gently and waited for a few moments before Q opened the front door. Q's eyes were bloodshot red and I could smell the liquor seeping through his pores.

"What's up?" Q shielded his eyes from the sunlight.

"I just wanted to come over and check on you. I know the last time we saw each other, I put my hands on you and I was wrong for that. I apologize."

"You good... come in," Q opened the door to allow me to gain entry. "I wanted to talk to you anyways. I know I was also out of pocket the last time we saw each other. I said some shit I meant, but I said it the wrong way."

"So you meant to be that damn rude to me?"

"No, just let me explain," Q pulled me over to the couch where we took a seat. "I have been battling with the idea of telling you what I overheard a while back, and I'm only telling you now so you can make your next move based off of all the facts. The day everybody was looking for you, I overheard Doe, Meechie, and Moochie talking. Doe confessed to leaving the club with a stripper that night your cousin saw him there."

"Ain't no way... Moochie would have told me some shit like that," I quickly pulled away from Q. "I can't believe you would stoop so low. I'm with Doe and that's that. We are getting married. I came over here to check on you out of the kindness of my heart and you sitting here trying to throw dirt," I hopped up from the couch.

"You think I would lie about some shit like that?"

"If it's the truth, then why tell me now? You wait until the moment I say I'm not trying to be fucked up with you to tell me this? What sense does that make?"

"This is exactly why I never told you. I didn't want you to look at me like I was on some fuck shit," Q's anger now matched mine. "I've kept it realer than your own fiancé! You believe that nigga over me? Cool."

"You damn right I do," I yelled back. "This is the last time you will *ever* see me on a personal tip," I stormed out of the house.

I clicked the button on my key fob to unlock my doors.

"Jayla?" I heard my name being called from across the street before

LAKIA

I opened the door. I looked up and noticed Cheeky at the mailbox with a handful of letters.

"Cheeky! What's up girl?" I plastered a fake grin on my face because Q had my blood pressure up.

"Shit, girl... long time no see."

"Things have been crazy to say the least," I noted.

"What you doing over here? How do you know that fine ass chocolate God who stays over there?" Cheeky inquired as she crossed the street.

"Oh that's my cousin," I quickly asserted.

"Well shit, is your cousin single? We haven't formally met, but I've seen that dick print through those grey sweats, so I'd like to get to know him for sure," Cheeky licked her lips, oblivious to the fact that she was gawking over a nigga that I'd never hand over to her.

"Nah, he's not single," I answered flatly.

"I'm still waiting for you to hook me up with a date," Cheeky reminded me.

"Girl, I'm glad you said that. Our wedding was pushed up to next Saturday. I'm going to send you the details."

"Oh wow! What's the rush? Are you pregnant?" Cheeky pressed her hands against my flat stomach.

"Hell no! My man actually surprised the hell out of me last night. He threw a little party and announced that he moved our wedding date up. He even planned everything while I been running around here giving him my ass to kiss," I confessed.

"I definitely need you to put me down with somebody asap. I don't want to show up alone," Cheeky mentioned.

"I got you, I have a cousin who needs a date. I am going to text you guys each other's information so y'all can link up. I can only put you in the game, I can't get you the position though."

"I ain't never had a problem securing a position. This is right on time too... my nigga I was dealing with just left me after being together for a year. No use crying over spilled milk though, just *put me in the game coach*," Cheeky laughed.

"Jayla!" I heard Q calling my name from the doorstep.

"I gotta go," I waved to Cheeky before rushing to my car. I locked the doors as Q knocked on my windows. I didn't have shit to say to his ass. The moment Cheeky was out of the way, I backed out of the driveway and sped off.

I made it a few blocks before Q swerved his car in front of mine. It was like déjà vu all over again, except this time, it was Q blocking me.

22

Q

I threw back another shot after Jayla stormed out of the house. If she wanted to be with that cheating ass nigga, that was on her. I poured another shot as I heard Jayla's voice yapping with somebody else in the yard. After throwing back a second shot, I rushed out of the house. Jayla took off as soon as I called her name, but she didn't get far before I cut her off in traffic.

"I don't have shit else to say Q," Jayla spoke through the car window.

"So you **really** done for real?

"Yes Q, I meant everything I said. Now please stop causing a scene and let me go," Jayla yelled through the door without ever taking her eyes off of the road.

The coldness in her eyes caused me to let her go about her business. I hopped in my car and headed back home.

"Hey neighbor, how do you know my good friend Jayla?" The woman sitting on the porch across the street yelled out to me.

She was being loud as fuck in this quiet neighborhood, so I decided to ignore her ass. Plus, fuck that bitch, or something along those lines were likely to roll off of the tip of my tongue. I went back into the house and initiated my day drinking. By eight o'clock, I was pissy drunk and out of my feelings as I exchanged freaky texts with Sheena. The liquor had me horny as fuck, and here I was, unable to bust a nut because the woman I spent my time on had a nigga. I was a whole duck behind closed doors for Jayla. I pushed my thoughts of Jayla out of my mind and got back into my phone. I snapped a picture of my dick and sent it to Sheena.

Me: He wishes you were here (smirking emoji).

Sheena: I'm coming home tomorrow for a week. You must be ready to let me sit on it again? (grinning emoji)

Me: You know it. Let me know when you touch down.

I laid my phone down and did something I hadn't done in a long time. I jacked my dick before I hopped in the shower and went to sleep. I woke up the next morning with a text from Sheena asking me to pick her up from the airport. Since I was in need of some relief, I quickly confirmed. After throwing on a pair of Levi jeans, a red Gucci shirt, and my red and white Jordan retro 9's, I headed to the shop to chop it up with Meechie and Doe.

"Nigga, what you all dressed up for?" Meechie questioned.

"He must got a new bitch already. I ain't never seen this boy out of his basketball shorts and a black tee. My boy got on a Gucci shirt and a pair of pants. I need to see the lady that got my boy getting dressed," Doe joked.

"Yeah man, I have been on the fence about rekindling an old flame, but I finally got the motivation to see what happens. She wasn't happy about me moving here and that's what messed us up, which is actually why I am here to talk to y'all. I'm out the game and moving away to get my life in order in after today," I notified them of my resignation.

"Fuck no Q! You gotta give us a little more notice than that," Meechie protested.

"I gotta do what I gotta do man," I informed them.

"Alright man, I get it, but you know I'm getting married Saturday. Then I'm going on a short little six day honeymoon. I can't leave this nigga to fend for himself," Doe mushed Meechie.

"Nigga," Meechie mushed him back playfully. "Nah, but for real Q, can you just give us two more weeks for my sake? I can't be over the muscle and the drugs."

"What about Beanie?" I inquired.

"Man, Beanie ain't been right since Raheem disappeared. Lowkey, he's the reason we need you. The nigga accused us of doing something to his brother because I fired him before he went missing. So he ain't been fucking with us like that, and we just want to be on our shit at all time," Doe informed me.

I was surprised to hear about the issue with Beanie because nobody ever mentioned it to me before. I debated whether or not I wanted to stick around for that extra two weeks of cash that I hadn't included in my exit plan.

"I'll triple your salary at this point. You're worth every penny," Doe persuaded me, and I couldn't turn it down.

"Alright man, but after you get back from your honeymoon, you better have a replacement for me," I retorted.

I dapped up Meechie and Doe before I left the spot and headed to the airport. I stopped at the Hilton and secured us a room. I wasn't sure if I wanted Sheena to know where I stayed just yet; she demonstrated how crazy she could get after our breakup. Once the room accommodations were secured, I headed to the airport to pick up Sheena.

Sheena stepped outside looking just as fine as she did the other day; only this time, the Miami sun was causing her skin to glow only adding to her beauty. I rushed over and grabbed Sheena's bags before walking her over to the car.

"You look beautiful," I complimented Sheena before I opened her car door.

"Thank you handsome," Sheena replied.

"Do you have anywhere you need to go first?"

"My mother cooked a nice dinner for us. She's excited to see you since it's been so long," Sheena informed me.

Hearing that she wanted to go to her mother's house completely put a damper on my mood. I loved Sheena's mother, but I didn't feel like we were in a space to be doing the family thing. I didn't know where things would go with us, and I wanted to have that in order before we started kicking it with each other's families again.

"I have to handle a few things," I lied. "I'm going to drop you off and you can Uber to the hotel."

"Hotel?" Sheena questioned.

"Yeah, I wanted to make shit romantic," I lied.

"Okay Q," Sheena sat back in her seat as I maneuvered through the airport traffic.

Thirty minutes later, I dropped Sheena off at her mother's house. I didn't have shit else to do, so I went home and watched the basketball game while I waited for Sheena to say she was headed to the hotel. I fell asleep on the couch and woke up to a call from Sheena.

"Hello," I answered the phone

"Hey, I'm wrapping things up here. I'm about to request an Uber, but you never told me which hotel we were staying in."

"Don't worry about the Uber. I'll be over there in twenty minutes."

"Okay. I will see you when you get here," Sheena disconnected the call.

I hopped up and headed over to pick up Sheena. When we got back to the hotel room, Sheena was exhausted. After we showered, she changed into pajamas and fell asleep while I ate the to-go plate she brought from her mother's house. After pulling off my clothes and showering, I climbed in bed behind Sheena. The familiar scent of her pomegranate and honey hair products invaded my nostrils as I pulled her into my chest. Sheena stirred from her sleep and turned around to face me. As bad as I wanted to fuck, I decided to fight the urge and placed a kiss on Sheena's forehead before she turned around.

The next few days went by without a hitch. We enjoyed each other's company without any arguments, so I decided to invite her to Doe and Jayla's rehearsal dinner. I didn't even want to attend the event, but Meechie and Doe pleaded with me. I actually started to feel bad for fucking ol' boy's old lady, but I had to save face and show up to these functions to avoid any further questions. With Sheena's crazy side in check, we finally took things to my house this morning.

Sheena was dressed in a thigh length blush off the shoulder dress and a pair of gold strappy heels. I was wearing a red Polo button up, some slacks, and a pair of Gucci loafers.

"The light in your bathroom is trash," Sheena walked out of the bathroom with a hand held mirror and her makeup bag in her hand.

"Try the kitchen," I suggested as Sheena exited the bedroom.

"What about this room?" I heard Sheena jingling with the second bedroom that was remodeled for Jayla.

"Hol' up!" I came rushing down the hallway.

"What's this?" Sheena was already in the room before I could reach her.

"Nothing," I attempted to push Sheena out of the room.

"This is a whole lot more than *nothing*. This room is decorated better than any room in this house. You had another bitch living here?"

"Nah, and don't start that shit Sheena," I voiced.

"Damn, I can't inquire about this prissy ass room in your house? I mean, do you need to tell me something? Are you using this shit? Let me find out..."

"Man, don't fucking play with me," I responded. "I did all of this for the girl I was seeing. That's it."

"Must be nice. Well she isn't in your life anymore so the least you can let me do is touch up my makeup in here," Sheena re-entered the room.

I watched Sheena apply her makeup and laughed to myself. I did all of this shit for Jayla and she never even put this room to use. Hell, Sheena might as well use it. I retreated back into the bedroom and sprayed on a little cologne and went back to the living room to wait for Sheena. Another ten minutes went by and Sheena was still in the makeup room.

"You already got us running late trying to freak me Sheena," I called out.

I wasn't complaining though, Sheena gave me the relief that I desperately needed, and I was feeling refreshed.

"I'm coming," Sheena walked out of the makeup room looking beautiful as always.

I grabbed her hand and led her to the car. The wedding rehearsal was held at Doe and Jayla's house; however, I wasn't in the wedding so we were just making a quick appearance at the dinner party afterwards. Doe really had pulled all the stops out tonight as we dropped my car off with the valet and headed inside. I gripped Sheena's hands in mine as we walked into the house. The oversized dining room now housed two enormous tables with enough seats for the wedding party and a few of the other fellas from the team and their women. Since we were running late, everyone was already seated and eating, so I quickly said what's up to a few people before we found my place card and took a seat.

"So you're Mrs. Q?" Meechie walked over and greeted us.

"In this flesh," Sheena smiled.

"Nigga, you ain't going to introduce us to your girl?" Meechie nudged me.

"My bad, she had us running late and shit so I'm all out of whack. Everybody, this is my girl Sheena," I announced to everyone at our table.

Honestly, I hadn't introduced her because I didn't expect this to be an intimate sit down meal. I thought everyone would be mingling in the backyard like the last few events. I avoided eye contact with Jayla the entire time we were there and waiting for our food. I was relieved when the door opened again and in walked the nosy ass bitch who lived across the street from me with some dude on her arm. Doe started coughing uncontrollably and Jayla rubbed his back before she stood up.

"Everyone, this is my homegirl Cheeky. She hooked me up with the plug on the hair so I invited her," Jayla cheered before embracing Cheeky with a hug.

I noticed the evil glares Jayla sent my way before she reclaimed her seat next to her king. The waiter brought out the chicken, rice pilaf, and asparagus plates for the four late comers. I took a few bites before my phone buzzed, alerting me to a text message.

J: I swear to God if we weren't in a room full of people I would beat your ass right now! How the fuck you going to walk in here with another bitch on your arm? You got me fucked all the way up Q!

Me: (crying laughing emoji) As you sit next to your future husband, you worried about who I got on my arm. LOL. Mrs. Jones have a nice life. I know I will. You chose your king.

23

DOE

I damn near choked on the water I was sipping out of the glass when Cheeky entered the room. I just knew my mind was playing tricks on me. My eyes connected with Meechie's as we silently communicated with each other. When Jayla hopped up, my heart sank to the pit of my stomach as I watched Jayla embrace Cheeky. If we weren't in a room full of my elder family members, I would have put one right through Cheeky's skull. She knew she was playing a dirty game, and she just didn't give a fuck. Jayla suddenly got quiet and wasn't as bubbly as she had been the entire night, which was starting to concern me. I started to wonder if Jayla had any idea about my history with Cheeky.

"I don't feel so well," Jayla got up and excused herself from the table.

I stood to follow Jayla, but Moochie jolted from her seat before I could. I sat back down and played around with my food while engaging in bits and pieces of conversations when I could. Every time I looked up from my plate, Cheeky was giving me a seductive glance, but she just didn't know the last thing I wanted to do was give her some dick. I really wanted to strangle this bitch on the middle of the table.

My daydream of choking the life out of Cheeky was cut short when

I noticed Tammy and Ms. Jennifer head to the back where Jayla and Moochie were. I excused myself from the table and headed in that direction as well.

"You think she's having a panic attack?" I could hear Tammy question as I headed down the hallway.

"No, I'm okay..." Jayla sounded like she was out of breathe.

"Jayla, if you don't want to marry Doe, then don't. If you are having cold feet, tell the nigga to pump the breaks and go back to the original wedding date while you think about your decision," Moochie spoke.

"I'm okay y'all," Jayla spoke as I appeared in the doorway.

Everyone was fanning Jayla, and if looks could kill, my own cousin would be dead for that dumb ass shit I heard her spitting.

"Can I have a moment with my woman?" I questioned, stroking my beard.

Everyone silently cleared the room for Jayla and me.

"Aye man, me and Q about to head out," Meechie spoke from over my shoulder.

I turned to dap the both of them up before they departed the party, and I wished they would tell everybody else to follow suit.

"You good Jayla?" I questioned.

"I'm okay Doe. I told them I was fine," Jayla stood from the chair. "Just let me touch up my makeup and I'll be right out. You know today has been a long and tiring day. I guess this was my bridezilla moment."

"You sure?" I questioned.

"I'm positive babe," Jayla planted a kiss on my lips before she walked into the bathroom and finished fixing her makeup.

When we returned to the party, everybody was packing up and conversing. Jayla and I started thanking people for coming out as they exited our home. Once we were alone and the cleaning crew had our place back in order, I swept Jayla off of her feet and carried her to the bedroom after locking up.

I ran Jayla a warm bubble bath while she undressed. Jayla's naked body was flawless as her dress met the floor. I wanted to take her right there, but I knew she just had a really emotional and draining day. Plus she suggested that we waited a few more days until our wedding night to make it seem a little special--Jayla's idea, not mine. But I jumped onboard because I was willing to do anything to fix us. Once I helped Jayla into the tub, I could hear my phone chiming on the dresser back to back.

"Let me go make sure everything is straight," I informed Jayla before I walked back into the bedroom.

There were a few messages from Cheeky. All ranting and shit as if I gave a damn. The one message that caught my eye had me infuriated.

Cheeky: After seeing your house I have made the executive decision to keep the baby. I ain't stripping no more so you need to make sure I have enough money to cover my expenses on the first. I hope the Mrs. is ready to welcome me and the baby to the family. #JoiningTheJoneses baby daddy!

I threw my phone down and stomped on it twice since I really wanted to be stomping Cheeky's ass out, that would have to do. I sat on the bed and ran my hands down my face while I took a few deep breaths.

"Is everything okay baby?" Jayla questioned, wrapping the towel around her waist.

"I'm good. I'm just ready to shower and go to bed."

"What happened to your phone?" Jayla noticed the dismembered phone on the floor.

"Nothing for you to worry about. I'm going to grab a new phone in the morning. Are you going to wait up for me while I jump in the shower?"

"I'm going to try Doe, but I'm exhausted," Jayla answered, rubbing body butter down her legs.

24

JAYLA

Our wedding was less than 24 hours away and I was sitting in Bianca's chair getting my new bundles installed, so I would be ready for my big day. Cheeky also came up there to keep me company during the long process. After my hair was laid and not a single hair was out of place, I paid Bianca for her services and said goodbye to both of the ladies.

"Don't forget. Tomorrow, I need you there at noon," I reminded Bianca once I made it to the door.

"I won't forget, I will be there with bells on," Bianca sang.

When my ass touched the driver's seat, Moochie was calling my phone.

"Hello," I answered after connecting my phone to the bluetooth.

"I need a little more excitement in your voice bihhhhhh!" Moochie's voice bounced around in my car.

"I am excited and scared about what all you have planned," I chirped.

"Well you have an hour before you need to meet us at the hotel, Jayla. Please be on time. We have a tight schedule," Moochie beamed.

"I will be on time girl," I answered before disconnecting the call.

I headed home and packed my bag for the night. Doe reserved suites for the ladies at the Marriott on South Beach and the fellas were going to be staying at 1 Hotel South Beach. Doe entered the house with his tuxedo in hand as I carried my duffle bag down the stairs.

"I got it bae," Doe threw his tux across the table by the entrance and rushed over to me.

"Thank you," I beamed, looking up at Doe.

Since Doe's accident, it was crazy how much he had changed. He was more attentive and always looking for ways to help me out and plaster a smile on my face.

"Anything for my wifey," Doe grabbed the bag from my hand. "Are you leaving now?"

"No, I have a few minutes before I need to meet the ladies at the hotel."

"Alright," Doe placed my bag next to the door.

"What time are you leaving?"

"Right after you," Doe placed a kiss on my lips.

"What are you guys getting into tonight?" I inquired.

"You know Meechie planned everything."

"I know there will be strippers involved tonight Doe. Just don't make me leave you standing alone tomorrow," I expressed, meaning every word I said.

"I won't Jayla. I have really been putting forth the effort to make us work. You have got to see the changes taking place in me," Doe expressed.

"I recognize it," I responded. "But you have a checkered past so sometimes I feel like you need reminding."

"I promise you never have to worry about that kind of shit again. You just make sure you're ready to give me all of *this* tomorrow night. I don't even want to attend the reception. I want to skip straight to fucking on you," Doe's hands roamed my body and his tongue invaded my mouth.

Doe was my first, and he was truly the only one who I was sexually comfortable with. The sexual exploitations I had with Q were light compared to the things I had done with Doe. I ran my fingers through Doe's beard as I sucked on his tongue, and Doe mashed my body into his with his forearm.

"Okay, okay," I broke away from his embrace before I ended up late to the hotel.

"You need to just give me a quickie for good luck bae," Doe pleaded before sucking on my neck.

"Stop Doe," I chuckled. "You will have all of this soon enough," I flicked my tongue against Doe's earlobe. "Now I need to go. I know that ain't nobody but Moochie who has my phone buzzing so much."

"They can wait Jayla," Doe put on his sexiest voice. "I bet Moochie got fucked this morning so she can understand. Plus they will have you all night," Doe wrapped me up in his arms and planted a few kisses on my neck as he continued to plead his case.

"I'm leaving Doe," I pulled all the way out of Doe's grasp and strutted to the door.

"Alright man," Doe slapped my ass and grabbed my bag from the floor.

I kissed him one final time before I proceeded to the hotel. I wasn't too late because Tammy and my cousins Jordan and Fallon were standing at the desk checking in as well.

"Y'all ladies ready for some fun!" Moochie's loud ass emerged from the elevator with a bottle of Armand de Brignac Ace of Spades Rose in hand. All eyes were on Moochie as she drunk straight from the bottle. "I have y'all key cards already. Let's go!" Moochie continued to be loud as hell.

"Damn bitch, pipe down," Tammy jeered once the elevator closed.

"It's my bitch wedding weekend. I'm here for her every day, you're only around when it's convenient. Excuse me if I'm a little more invested in this monumental event in her life," Moochie stepped towards Tammy and Tammy didn't back down.

"Both of y'all relax!" I chimed in and the elevator doors opened.

"I'm calm Jay, you better tell your lil friend about me," Moochie stepped off of the elevator.

"That's all of the shit talking y'all are going to do this weekend!" I yelled in the hallway. "Please, this weekend is about me."

"I'm sorry," Tammy and Moochie sang in unison.

"That's more like it," I followed Moochie down the hallway.

Jordan and Fallon were my only female cousins, but they were prissy as hell so I wasn't surprised when they just stood there looking embarrassed. Fallon was a doctor and Jordan worked as a nurse at her office. They were not about that life like the rest of us, but I still loved them the same. Moochie led us to the larger suite where I would be staying for the evening.

"Alright y'all, get dressed," Moochie instructed. "We are club hopping and all types of shit tonight."

Everyone went back to their rooms to get changed and we were dressed and meeting in the lobby within thirty minutes. I was dressed in a teal fringe romper that Doe bought me last week for this special occasion. The romper hugged every curve of my body, and I felt my ass jiggle with every step in this outfit. I threw on the black Christian Louboutin heels and grabbed the black and teal Chanel clutch that Doe purchased for me as well. My baby really did his thang putting this ensemble together. My girls entered the lobby looking just as fine as me in a variety of colors and labels.

"First things first, we have a car service. So Jayla, throw on this little *bride to be* crown," Moochie opened the box to her childish prop and handed it to me. I didn't protest. I fell in line and placed it on my head.

"Where are we going?" I questioned as we piled into the back of the limousine.

"Shhhhhhh," Moochie shoved a shot in my face and I graciously accepted it. "First stop is dinner so y'all won't be getting sick and shit," Moochie notified the group before the driver pulled away from the curb.

We drove all of 300 feet before the car stopped in front of Prime 112, and I couldn't help but cackle at Moochie's antics. We could have walked over for all of that.

"What? Everybody in heels and shit. We were not about to walk over here. Plus we will be leaving here and going straight to our next destination. I told you, we are on a tight schedule," Moochie addressed my persistent giggling.

"For the first time, I'm with Moochie. I didn't mind the ride over," Tammy voiced and exited the car once the driver opened the door.

"Me either. Jordan picked out these pumps I can barely walk in," Fallon wobbled out of the car.

When we entered the restaurant and took our seats, Moochie immediately waived down the waiter so we could place our food and drink orders. I chose the jumbo lump crab crusted grouper with wilted spinach. We enjoyed the delectable food while we laughed about various events from our past.

"I remember when Jayla used to curb all of the dudes in high school and college so she could focus on her studies," Jordan laughed.

"Yessssss, I was on track to become a doctor but even I would enjoy myself. Jayla used to be an old Judge Judy ass bitch," Fallon added.

"She must have done something right, she is the only one out of the click with a fiancé," Tammy added in.

"Shit she's the *only* one with a man, period," Moochie laughed as she passed the waiter a few bills to cover the tab we ran up.

"Y'all just going to keep talking shit like I'm not right here?"

"Yes girl, if you haven't noticed, we are doing a lowkey roasting session in your face," Moochie notified me. "Now, are y'all ready to go on our next adventure?"

"Yes," I answered quickly, ready to get away from the chatter of my past.

"Let's go!" Moochie yelled out, causing her second scene of the night.

We quickly followed Moochie back out to the limo and piled inside.

"Now everyone pass these shots down until we all have one," Moochie started doling out shots of vodka while we re-entered traffic.

After the thirty minute drive and countless shots, we pulled up in front of King of Diamonds. I quickly glanced at Moochie because I damn sure wasn't trying to look at naked bitches all night.

"Relax, this next part of the night was not designed by me," Moochie answered the questions that were swirling around in my head.

Before I could respond to Moochie, the door to the limousine opened and there stood my bearded king in the flesh.

"I promised you that there would be no more clubbing, no more partying, no more drinking unless you're on my arm, so these next two hours you're here with me," Doe affirmed before gripping my hand and helping me step out of the car.

"Take charge then cousin!" Moochie cheered Doe on.

Doe placed a kiss on my lips before grabbing my hand and leading our group into the club.

"Awwwwwww shit! Congratulations are in order for my nigga Doe and his future wife Jayla!" the DJ yelled over the speakers as we walked inside.

Doe dapped up a few of the fellas as we made our way to the area that was setup for our group. There were bottles of every type of liquor in our section, and we all started throwing back drinks. I couldn't lie; my mood had changed for the better since we pulled up in the parking lot. I didn't mind being in the strip club with Doe. I knew the fellas wanted to do the traditional strippers before the wedding night routine, but I was over the moon at the realization that Doe was taking his promise to me serious. Doe and Moochie passed out stacks of ones for everyone to throw around, and I indulged in a few lap dances with Doe. I was lit after an hour of partying with the fellas. I grabbed the bottle from the bucket of ice and drank straight from the bottle, taking a direct page out of Moochie's book. She was turnt up to the max, so I was trying to get like her tonight.

There was a fine ass redbone with the perfect pair of pierced nipples strutting around in our section, and I motioned for her to come over and put on a show for us. As the stripper bent over and shook her ass in Doe's face, I stood up and placed my last stack of cash in one hand and used the other hand to flick the cash over the woman and her perfect body as City Girls *Twerk* serenaded the atmosphere. When the song was over, the woman collected her cash and exited our section with her earnings in hand. Doe took a pull from the blunt Meechie passed his way and leaned over the seat to blow a shotgun to my face. In that moment, all I could think about were our younger days and how far we had come.

"I wish you would give in and come back to the room with me tonight," Doe pulled me in his lap and whispered in my ear. "I dressed you for the night, it's only right that I tear it off of yo fine ass."

Doe's hands roamed my body as he sucked on my earlobe. Doe was just about to convince me with my liquor hazed mind until Cheeky entered our section wearing a thong bikini and the tallest pair of clear heels I had ever seen. After conversing with Cheeky for the past few weeks, I never knew she was a stripper. But I didn't judge; I supported all hustles.

"Cheeky!" I waved Cheeky over just as Meechie grabbed her arm.

"Jayla!" Cheeky beamed once we locked eyes, and she walked over with all of the confidence in the world. "I don't even feel right dancing in front of you and that fine ass man of yours. It's nice to see you again," Cheeky waived at Doe, and he nodded his head to say what's up.

"Here girl, these niggas over here got cake," I handed Cheeky a stack with the band still wrapped around it. "You better go get you a few lap dances," I cheered her on.

Cheeky walked off to work the crowd until Meechie informed us that it was time to head to our next destination. I was ready to go home and go to bed. My stomach didn't feel the best after all of the liquor I had consumed, but I was still lit as Doe gripped my waist and pulled me into him once we met the night air. I drunkenly kissed Doe as he gripped my ass and quickly rubbed his hand over my kitty through my clothes, only making me want to ditch the girls even more.

"Aht aht! Break that shit up!" Moochie yelled across the parking lot. "Come on Jayla, I done already heard this nigga ask you to leave with him a few times. Ugh nope, not going to happen!"

"You heard my bestie," I pulled out of Doe's embrace and followed Moochie to the limo as Doe called my name.

I spun around and blew Doe a kiss before I joined the rest of the ladies in the car.

"Next stop Club Lexx!" Moochie announced once the driver closed the door.

After thirty minutes of twerking and drinking there, we had to cut the night short because Fallon's prissy ass couldn't handle her liquor and was barely able to stand on her own two feet. The moment we got Fallon to her hotel room, she started that throwing up shit.

LAKIA

"Since it's my big day tomorrow, y'all need to stay here and handle her," I informed the rest of the ladies before I quickly exited the room.

I just received a text that had me in my feelings and I needed to go.

25

DOE

The moment Cheeky walked into our section, I was livid. I was happy that Jayla cut it short with her ass. I made it clear to Meechie to let the owners know that if we were buying out the bar, she wasn't to be in attendance. We could have chosen a different strip club to avoid all of that. I wanted to take Jayla back to my room and fuck her brains out, but Moochie was cock blocking like she never had before. After the women were gone, I made a beeline to Meechie.

"What the fuck was she even doing here tonight?!" I based over the music.

"I don't know. We told that nigga to make sure she wasn't here tonight," Meechie threw his hands up. "She didn't cause a scene though."

"Y'all talking about little old me?" Cheeky planted her ass between the both of us.

"Get the fuck up Cheeky!" I barked and drug Cheeky out of the section by her arm and towards the bathrooms so she could hear me loud and clear.

"Ouch!" Cheeky yelped, attempting to release the vice grip I had on her arm.

"What the fuck are you doing here?" I inquired once we were in a better place for Cheeky to hear and feel me.

"I just had one of my homegirls open the backdoor. Did you think I was going to miss the party that MY baby daddy was throwing? Nah, if the rest of these bitches were going to get fed off of your dime, then so am I," Cheeky retorted.

"We are *done* Cheeky! I don't give a fuck if you keep this baby or not. I ain't taking care of your raggedy ass! I'll look out for my jit, but fuck you! If you show up at my wedding tomorrow, your ass ain't walking out of that bitch, pregnant or not. Play with me like I'm pussy if you want to, I can guarantee you that! Try me Cheeky!" I vexed directly in Cheeky's face so she could see just how serious I was.

I was done playing nice to keep the peace with her ass. Once Jayla was my wife, it would be harder for her to leave, and I'm sure we could get through this because this would be my last fuck up. I was positive about that. Cheeky taught me a valuable lesson, why fuck with these thots when I have a queen who would go to the end of the earth for me at home? Cheeky cowered under my evil glares. I prayed that meant she got the hint and understood where I was at with it. Cheeky quickly ran off, hopefully towards the dressing room so she could get the fuck on so that me and my niggas could enjoy the rest of my night.

"I apologize," the owner approached our area. "I sent Cheeky home. She won't be a problem for you gentlemen this evening. Thank you for your business."

After another hour of smoking, drinking, and lap dances, we all headed back to the hotel. Some of the fellas brought back some strippers, but I wanted no parts. I wasn't about to fuck up tonight. When I got back to my hotel room, I took a warm shower and laid down in the bed. I wasn't drunk, but the liquor and all of the last minute errands that I ran had my ass tired. I pulled out my phone as I felt my eyes getting heavier and called Jayla. Since she didn't answer, I figured the ladies were still out turning up. With Moochie in charge, I just prayed they all didn't look like hell tomorrow. I decided to pour out my heart to Jayla before sleep consumed me.

Me: I love you with everything in me. I know I've fucked up

on countless occasions but you never turned your back on me. For that, I owe you the world and you shall receive just that. I love you unconditionally! -Your future husband Doe.

26

Q

I stared at my phone for hours tonight as I typed, deleted, and retyped at least fifty different messages to Jayla. I wanted her to be happy, and I wanted to leave her the fuck alone. But the moment Sheena left town yesterday, Jayla was the only thing on my mind, which let me know that I wasn't ready to move on. Sheena deserved better so I didn't plan to lead her on any further. I threw back another double shot of Hennessy on the couch, and the liquor really had me feeling myself as I finally decided to hit send on my last message I typed. The shit I decided to send was nothing compared to all of the previous heartfelt messages I typed on my keyboard.

Me: Before you get married can we fuck one more time.

I followed that message up with a link to the classic Plies song *1 Mo Time*. I grabbed the Hennessy bottle and threw back another shot. My phone rang and to my surprise, Jayla was calling.

"Hello," I answered the phone.

"You going to come pick me up?" Jayla question, cutting straight to the point and for once, I didn't even mind. I accepted the fact that I was the nigga she called when her man didn't treat her right.

"I'm fucked up, but I'll send an Uber to you... send me your address," I placed Jayla on speaker phone and request an Uber.

"I'm sending it to you now."

Jayla's location came through on the phone, and I hopped up to grab a bottle of wine that I bought for Jayla the night I thought she was moving in and placed it in the freezer for it to chill faster.

"The Uber is on the way," I notified Jayla after we sat in an awkward silence for a few minutes.

"You know what? I can just drive to you because I don't want the hassle of figuring out how I will get back later."

"Alright, I'll see you when you get here."

I cancelled the Uber and rushed around the house straightening up the place and looking for any signs of Sheena. After collecting the few items Sheena left behind, I threw them in the dumpster outside. I saw that loud ass girl from across the street rushing to her front door emitting loud ass ugly sobs. I stole a glance at her wearing a bikini and no shoes in the night air and kept it moving. Once the house was together, I hopped in the shower and got my hygiene together before I threw on a pair of Polo boxers and pajama pants that Jayla bought me when we first met. I grabbed a few candles I had from the linen closet and placed them around the bedroom.

The light knocks at the door jolted me from the couch as I rushed over to get the door for Jayla. Jayla stood there looking good enough to devour whole. She still had that weave in and her curves were still present through her tan peacoat. I stepped aside and allowed Jayla to cross the threshold. I wasn't sure how to go about this because the last time Jayla texted me, she was ready to beat my ass for bringing Sheena to her rehearsal dinner.

I locked the door and turned around. Jayla dropped her peacoat, exposing her naked body underneath. Initially, I was pissed that she came outside this late like that, niggas was crazy in these streets. Since this would be our last encounter, I decided to keep my mouth shut. I just wanted to feel the sensation that both sets of lips gave me one more time.

Jayla strutted over to me in complete silence, and I could taste the liquor mixed with Colgate on her tongue. I lifted Jayla off of her feet, and she pulled her heels off before I carried her to the bed. I tossed Jayla's frame onto the bed, and I roughly put all of my weight on top of her before I roughly shoved my tongue down her throat. I gripped Jayla's ass and put her in position before I grabbed a condom off of the night stand and slid it on.

I drilled in and out of Jayla, causing her to squeal out as she scratched my back. Although I was being rough and ensuring that Jayla felt all of my emotions through the rough sex we were engaging in, she was getting equally as rough. I felt the skin breaking on my back from Jayla's acrylic nails, causing me to wince in pain slightly. I flipped Jayla over and gripped her weave as I entered her from behind. I had Jayla's weave wrapped around my left hand as I gripped her waist with my right hand. Jayla didn't falter; she was still throwing it back just as hard as I was giving it to her. We were both under the influence and pissed with each other, so it made for a long round of rough sex. Afterwards, we both climaxed together.

"I love you Q," Jayla broke the silence in the room after we finally caught our breath. "I'm sorry that we didn't meet under different circumstances. You are a good man and I am positive you will find an amazing woman, and from this day forward, I won't hate on that. I want to see you happy."

Although Jayla's words stung, I could respect the honesty.

"I love you too Jayla," I softened up and pulled her into my chest. "When y'all get back from your lil honeymoon, I'm moving back to Tallahassee to finish school earlier than I anticipated, so you don't have to worry about seeing me around anymore after tomorrow and don't worry... your secret is safe with me."

I went into the bathroom and wiped my dick off before retrieving the bottle of Hennessy from the couch. I took a few swigs before I reentered the room. I sat on the edge of the bed and Jayla crawled over to me without speaking a word. After drinking straight from the bottle, Jayla pulled a condom from the box on the nightstand.

Jayla ripped the condom open with her teeth and gave my dick a few licks, causing me to instantly get hard. I wanted to pressure her for some head, but I knew she had to kiss that nigga tomorrow and probably wouldn't go for it, so I accepted the few licks before she mounted me and slid down my dick. Jayla used her feet to assist her in riding me in that position. I leaned back and gently flicked her clit, causing Jayla to pick up her pace. I stood from the bed and picked Jayla up without letting my dick slip out of her wet center. I locked Jayla's right foot and right arm into my left arm and did the same with the other leg and foot and fucked her in that standing position, giving me complete control until she was calling my name just before she creamed all over my dick. I released my seeds into the condom moments later and allowed Jayla's legs to meet the floor again. Jayla climbed in bed and fell asleep instantly. I hopped in the shower and got cleaned up while I thought about everything that had transpired since I met Jayla. As sad as I was for this road to come to an end, it probably was for the best.

27

JAYLA

I woke up the next morning with my stomach in knots; my nerves had the absolute best of me. That feeling only intensified when the realization of last night settled in. After getting pissy drunk and dipping off with Q for the rest of the night, I woke up in his arms and in a panic. I told myself last night was the last time, and it was going to be a quickie before I drove over to his house. But the moment I stepped into his attempt at a romantic setup and had a little more Hennessy, we ended up fucking until I fell asleep. Sore was an understatement for how my yoni felt.

I checked the clock and instantly hopped up from the bed. It was already one o'clock; our wedding started at six o'clock and I was supposed to be back at the house before noon. I quickly showered and gathered my things, leaving Q in the bed asleep. I didn't want to wake him for fear of starting some shit today. When I arrived at the house, I looked like shit. I was slightly hungover, my bundles smelled like liquor and weed, and I could barely walk right. The rough sex was a pleasant surprise because Q had always been so gently with me. Now that I was sober, I knew Q's ass wanted to be all rough and shit just so I could feel like this today. I stepped into the house with my oversized shades still protecting my eyes from the brightness of the sun and now the lights in the house. The moment that Moochie laid eyes on me, she started talking shit.

"Bitch, where the fuck you been? I have been lying to Doe since he got here an hour ago! Get your raggedy ass in the chair and get yourself together quick because you look like shit," Moochie ranted, pulling me towards the dressing room. "Where the fuck did you even sneak off to? I was starting to think your ass was going to be a runaway bride. You left me with your drunk ass cousin throwing up all over the damn place. Oh, but don't worry. Doe is going to be the one paying for it when they hit him with that cleaning fee," Moochie continued to ramble, intensifying the headache that was already plaguing me.

"I... I... just needed some time alone. My nerves got the best of me. Hell, they are still getting the best of me," I mumbled before I started greeting everyone in the dressing room.

The entire time we prepared for the wedding was like a blur. I was zoned out while I got my hair, nails, and makeup done. My mind didn't rejoin my body until the bridesmaids walked down the aisle. I stood at the backdoor with my bouquet of coral roses embellished with Swarovski crystals in hand, internally shaking off any jitters that still lingered.

I could see all of the details I discussed with Draya come to fruition. I was thoroughly impressed that Doe went through all of the preparation on his own to impress me and marry me as fast as he could. My mother stood to my left in a coral dress that fit her perfectly and my father looked handsome in his black tuxedo with his coral tie. Although, I tried to convince my father to wear something less traditional since the weather was going to be in the mid seventies today.

Once the bridesmaids and groomsmen were in place, my mother and father locked their arms into mine, and we slowly strutted down the aisle once we received our cuc from the wedding planner. My mother and father both kissed me on the cheek after the reverend asked who gives this woman to be married to this man. Doe turned to me and gently gripped my hand and helped me up the few steps, so we were standing across from each other.

"Dearly beloved..."

The reverend started our vows, and I couldn't wait to get this shit over with. It wasn't that I wasn't happy, but a bitch was still fucked up from all of the liquor I consumed last night. I don't know who started the tradition of the bachelor and bachelorette party the night before the wedding, but that shit was ludicrous or had never been married. I tuned the entire speech out as I focused on keeping the smile plastered on my face to hide the fact that my mind was focused on the flashbacks from last night.

"If any of you has a reason why these two should not be married, speak now or forever hold your peace," the reverend looked out into the crowd and my eyes followed his.

Q stood to his feet for a brief second before he sat back down, and I pleaded with my eyes for him to sit the fuck down and to keep his mouth shut for both of our sakes. I didn't know who was or who wasn't carrying a gun today . But one thing I did know for sure was I damn sure wasn't trying to become well versed in that topic today.

"This shit all fucked up!" Q stood up again, slurring his words. In that moment, I knew he was fucked up and shit was about to go all the way left! I attempted to pull my hand out of Doe's because baby, I was planning to kick these heels off and make a run for it. However, I couldn't run because Doe's grip tightened as his eyes darted between Q and me.

"Nigga, sit yo drunk ass down," Meechie barked and shot Q a death glare. I had known Meechie most of my life, and I don't ever think I saw him this infuriated.

"Nah, I gotta speak my truth out this bitch," Q continued his belligerent rant and all of the older churchgoers in attendance clutched their pearls and gasped as if they never heard a few curse words in their life.

"What is you doing?" Meechie threw his arms up in the air and called out from next to Doe.

"Jayla been fucking around on you Doe," Q informed everyone in attendance.

"Nigga what?" Doe yelled out.

"I know she been fucking around because *I* been fucking Jayla since May and the baby she is carrying might be mine!" Q divulged, shocking the hell out of me and everybody else in attendance. Yeah I was fucking Q, but I *wasn't* pregnant. I guess he decided to go big or go home.

Meechie charged Q at full speed and Doe's hands instantly went to my neck. I ain't never been choked by anybody, so this shit was new to me and caught me completely off guard. I clawed at Doe's hands while I gasped for air. I could see my father rushing the stage and snuffing Doe, but Doe was so infuriated that he didn't budge from the shot to the jaw. In return, Doe's mother slapped my father across the back of the head with her purse and my mother retaliated by yanking Ms. Moni back by her wig. Ms. Moni's big ass purse must have had bricks or some shit in it because it left my father bleeding out the side of his head profusely.

A few of my male cousins from the crowd rushed the stage and attempted to free me from Doe's grasps. Before they could reach me, all of the groomsmen joined in on the action and were exchanging blows with my cousins.

"Bitch, you fucking a worker?!" Doe fumed with spit flying everywhere. "You been giving a worker my pussy! That is his baby because you ain't fucked me since you ran off in May."

Tammy rushed over from her spot on the stage next to me and tried to pry Doe's hands from around my neck, but he released me with his right hand momentarily to throw a punch to Tammy, sending her flying off of the stage. Tammy laid unconscious in the grass and Doe returned the right hand to my neck.

My wedding had turned into a free for all project fight. My mother was still fighting with Ms. Moni, Q and Meechie were going blow for blow, and I could see that Moochie had jumped in to help Meechie. Q got in one good punch on Moochie and knocked her wig to the left and her body to the right, only making Meechie pick up one of the chairs, bashing Q across the head with it before he fell to the floor. Meechie didn't stop there; he continued to bash Q across the back with the pieces of the chair that were still intact. Q did some ninja style move and swept his feet around, causing Meechie to fall on the ground with him. Q took that opportunity to hop on top of Meechie and rain blows to his face. Cousins, aunties, uncles, and friends from both sides were throwing hands everywhere. The poor children could be heard screaming over the obscenities that everyone was yelling at each other.

Fallon and Jennifer's bougie asses were rushing out of the backyard to escape the melee unscathed as I was on the brink of death and their uppity asses were probably the only ones close enough to help. Doe continued to choke me and yelled out questions I clearly couldn't answer with him crushing my windpipes. I started to make a gurgling sound and Doe didn't loosen his grip one bit. I could feel my life slipping away as I struggled to breathe. At first, I was trying to fight Doe off, but at this point, I was ready for the other side because this shit was ghetto as fuck!

TO BE CONTINUED ...

NOTE FROM THE AUTHOR

Thank you all for taking the time out to read my work. Jayla, Q and Doe will be back before you know it!

FOLLOW ME ON SOCIAL MEDIA:

INSTAGRAM @AuthorLakia
Facebook Author Lakia or Lakia Berrien

Join me in my Facebook group for giveaways, book discussions and a few laughs and gags! Maybe a few sneak peeks in the future. https://www.facebook.com/groups/keesbookbees

Or search Kee's Book Bees

AUTHOR LAKIA'S CATALOG

Surviving A Dope Boy: A Hood Love Story (1-3)
When A Savage Is After Your Heart: An Urban Standalone
When A Savage Wants Your Heart: An Urban Standalone
Trapped In A Hood Love Affair (1-2)
Tales From The Hood: Tampa Edition
The Street Legend Who Stole My Heart
My Christmas Bae In Tampa

Made in United States
Orlando, FL
31 March 2025